THE SPELL

by

C.V. Shaw

Published by Deletrea
www.deletrea.net

Author Photograph: Alexis Altarac   www.lexavellaphotography.com
Instagram: @lexavellaphotography

Cover Design: Karen Taylor   www.theartofkarentaylor.com
Instagram: @theartofkarentaylor

Layout Design: Mónica Candelas candelas.monica@outlook.com

Printed in the United States of America

"*The Spell* entrances with its twists and turns through enchanted and cursed territory. Against a fairytale backdrop, Shaw's tale unfolds through time, with complex and complicated characters and storylines, as Princess Isabella struggles to lift the "curse" of her pernicious family, eventually discovering the power of her own agency—and magic."

—Courtney E. Morgan, author of
The Seven Autopsies of Nora Hanneman

"With story lines that warn against focusing too much on the future and not enjoying the present, *The Spell* is a captivating fantasy novel...The novel blends elements of magical realism and historical fantasy in an intriguing way."

—*Clarion Review*

"A thought-provoking story that traces family relationships that evolve under a cloud of threat...Readers of romantic fantasy stories...will find *The Spell* truly captivating. It's a work that casts its own special magic on the reader's heart."

—*Midwest Book Review*

CB

Acknowledgment

I give thanks to the Divine Spirit of Love, who poured inspiration into my soul and also blessed me with my grandparents, Juancito and Mima, to whom I dedicate this book, as it was their magic tales that ignited my imagination.

LAKE BRIGHTONMERE

LUMIN WELLS

TOWN OF OPAL LAKE

GLASTONSHIRE

NORTH CUVINGTON

MULBERRY HILLS

SNOW QUEEN'S CASTLE

NOKBERSHIRE

CUVINGTON

BROTHER'S CROSS

ISLE OF BELFRONT

FLEURHAM

N
W   E
S

Chapter 1

It is the 16th century in England where, in the town of Fleurham—which borders the south edge of one of the countryside's lushest forests—sat a very old castle where King Maurice and Queen Lilac lived. The small town was nestled in the southeastern end of England and had survived a revolt with France. The king and queen were working their hardest to revive Fleurham, as tensions were still high among French inhabitants of the town.

Royal funds remained low and the rebuilding of Fleurham brought tension to the people of the castle, especially Lilac and Maurice, with Maurice being of French descent and Lilac of English. This caused disputes on both political and personal levels between them, leaving less than adequate attention for their five-year old daughter, Princess Isabella.

These tensions between them would temporarily subside, with Maurice passionately having his way with Lilac—and then they would start up again with quarreling when Maurice swiftly left Lilac's side to tend to his business—including philandering with the town's young maidens—leaving Lilac frustrated and lonely.

Maurice, a fiery, kingly man with a full, ashy blonde beard, bright blue eyes, and a deep voice, carried on with a calm demeanor and a magnetic charisma easy to envy. His nonchalant ways infuriated his often angry and controlling wife. She persistently nagged Maurice, driving him to explosive outbursts.

Their bickering was a noise the castle had become used to among the other day-to-day sounds.

The faint sound of workmen throughout the town could be heard through the red and yellow mosaic windows all around the castle. A light, constant thumping noise, almost hidden by the din of the workers, seemed unusual to Johndor. He knew the castle and its noises. Even if he was blind, he would have been able to keep up the castle. He held the mop still for a moment as he focused on the unfamiliar sound. Johndor had been the keeper of the castle at Fleurham for the last 10 years— since Lilac had moved there when she wed King Maurice. Lilac had agreed to marry Maurice under one condition—that she would bring Johndor, his wife Minna, and their daughters Lauren (who suffered from nervous tension) and Bethlynn (who had had her heart freshly broken), to keep the castle, as Lilac had practically been raised by the older couple.

Johndor glanced over at Minna, who stared blankly out the window at Peter, the peasant farmer delivering the chickens. Johndor ran his hand over his sparse salt-and-pepper hair as he began mopping again.

For a minute, it seemed Minna was trying to make out what Peter and Frances the cook were negotiating, but instead, Minna was actually trying to decipher an uneasy feeling she had about herself. Her tall, curvy body stood stiffer than usual.

Trying to figure out the distant sound, Johndor didn't notice Minna's absent-mindedness until she dropped the spoon she was polishing onto the silver platter, making a loud clanking sound and startling Minna back to reality. She looked to see Johndor's reaction and noticed he had set the mop against the wall and was walking with determination towards the stairs.

Minna wiped her hands on her white cotton apron and fixed the tight burgundy bun that sat atop her head as she walked out of the kitchen and followed Johndor down the hallway. She felt something was off, since Johndor had left the hallway half mopped. She paid close attention to Johndor's actions, as she well knew how astute he was and held a great deal of respect for the man. The tiny heels of her shoes clicked with every step behind him.

Johndor walked quickly and steadily despite a limp caused by his bowed knees, his face tense with a strict demeanor, his lips crooked from an old injury when a horse had thrown him off and proceeded to kick him in the mouth with its hind legs. He had many stories. You either believed them all or none. All were interesting, especially the one when a ghost jumped on the back of his horse. He claimed that when he turned to look, the ghost of a peasant with teeth as long as new pencils was smiling, demanding for his teeth to be looked at. "Lookamahteeth! Lookamahteeth!" Johndor would mimic, tucking in his chin to change his voice to a creepy, deep one.

Johndor finally reached the top step of the stone stairs, letting out a frustrated clicking of the tongue. Spotting Isabella, he rushed down the hallway and Minna hurried behind him. "I think she's had another nightmare." Johndor said looking back at Minna.

Isabella sat on the floor facing her parents' bedroom door, knocking nonstop, to a tune of three knocks and a pause.

"Why have they put you out?" Johndor asked, trying to ignore the sounds coming from behind the door. Isabella stared up at the enormous gilded wooden doors.

"Mother was crying funny, and it woke me. I think Papa was hurting her. I'm hungry."

Minna quickly picked Isabella up and whispered to Johndor, "They're carrying out another argument."

"Argument!" Johndor scoffed, shaking his head from side to side in disbelief. "The devil is wise because of his age, not his intelligence. That was no arguing, Minna," he said, still shaking his head with disgust at the sounds coming from the other side of the door.

Minna quickly cradled Isabella's head between her neck and chin to cover her ears as she carried her down the hall, patting her golden hair gently. Isabella let out a gentle whimper of sadness. Johndor clicked his tongue, shaking his head from side to side as he followed them back to the kitchen. The three walked slowly down the stone stairs, humming a lullaby. Isabella stretched out her hands, trying to graze the tapestry on the walls.

Johndor reached out and pulled Isabella's lower eyelids down to check her state of health. She then automatically stuck out her tongue, as she knew Johndor would be checking that next, to make sure her digestion was sound.

Chapter 2

King Maurice stormed out of his quarters while still fastening the buttons on his shirt. He yelled down the hallway to Samuel, the young manservant, who was straightening a wall tapestry, and ordered his foot soldiers to have his horses and horsemen made ready.

Queen Lilac, bitter at how Maurice always decided he needed some time away after he had romanced her, walked rapidly behind him. She held her head in frustration and angrily muttered, "You will be sorry. You will be sorry!"

Maurice spun and yelled, "Shut up, woman!" He grasped the nearest painting and slung it down the hall, shattering the golden frame.

Lilac's fingers curled, squeezing her thin strands of yellow hair tightly as she stomped her long legs faster after him.

Maurice took the stairs two at a time, his boots heavily echoing waves through the castle, trying to gain distance from Lilac's threats, which were reverberating behind him down the hallway.

Minna, who was still on her way downstairs, carrying Isabella, reached the bottom floor, where she heard the whispers of two ladies cleaning the library floors.

"He's certainly very angry," Lauren said. "I wonder what he broke this time."

"Wonder what she did this time?" Bethlynn responded. "That usually determines how much repair work there will be when he leaves."

"Oh, I hope it's not the painting of Isabella with her mother. Poor Samuel just repaired that one," Lauren said. "Lilac is lucky he has never reached for her face."

Bethlynn chimed in, "He's harmless at heart, but a little rearrangement to her face here and there might do her good." Lauren giggled, holding the duster to her belly.

Johndor, having accompanied Minna and Isabella down the stairs, continued to the kitchen as Minna excused herself and walked quickly to the library. She stood outside the door, leaned her head in and matter-of-factly said, "It's none of your business now, is it?" She cradled Isabella's head as the princess fought to unwind herself from Minna's hold after hearing her father yelling from the bottom of the stairs. Minna reached to firmly close the library doors shut just as Isabella escaped her grasp and took off running behind her father, out of the castle doors. Minna froze in confusion from all the mayhem.

Lilac, having just reached the bottom of the stairs, moved Minna out of the way and hurried after Isabella, shouting out to everyone, demanding that the princess be gathered and taken indoors. Johndor, having heard Lilac shouting, shuffled as quickly as he could out of the kitchen and through the castle doors after Isabella. He scooped her up mid-stride before she could catch up with the angry king, who was about to mount his horse. Johndor tried to lift her, but Isabella squealed when she heard her mother running outside and yelling at Maurice, demanding he get off his horse at once. She broke away from Johndor, kicking and screaming, and ran towards her mother. Before she could reach for her mother's waist, a black crow swooped down low at the princess's head, letting out a loud cackling sound. At the very same instant, an arrow darted from the west side of the forest, straight towards Isabella's little body. Startled, Isabella fell onto her mother, and both tumbled to the ground. The events happened so quickly and simultaneously that it was unclear whether the crow had provoked Isabella to fall or the arrow had shot the princess down.

A startled Maurice removed his foot from the stirrup and ran to their aid.

Lilac quickly sat up and cradled Isabella in her shaking arms. "Are you okay, my darling?" she asked, rocking the crying princess back and forth.

"I'm scared, Momma. I'm scared," she cried, looking at her scraped and bleeding hands and knees.

"After him!" King Maurice yelled at the horsemen. He then turned and yelled at Minna and Johndor, "Get them inside NOW!" Maurice stood staring into the forest, past the blanket of dirt kicked up from the racing horses making their way to find the mysterious archer.

The princess was quickly carried inside, Minna shielding Lilac as she clung to her crying daughter. Isabella grasped Minna's hand from her mother's shoulder, and gripped tightly to the fabric of her mother's gown with the other hand. Lilac laid her on her bed, her little hand remaining interlaced with Minna's. She refused to let go of either woman.

Johndor, having followed behind the women, looked over the squalling child and then excused himself to go find the leaves that would heal her scrapes and wounds, along with some leaves from the linden bushes to calm the princess down. Hastily, Johndor walked out of the castle, making his way towards the dense trees of the forest as he passed Maurice, who was standing with arms crossed and fixed like a soldier, guarding the edge of the woods. The king's voice escalated as Johndor continued to walk past him, advising Johndor to go back inside, as the archer could still be hidden somewhere within the trees. Johndor clicked his tongue as he whipped his head to the side in disobedience and walked straight into the deep forest with fearless determination. He emerged from the forest fifteen minutes later with soiled hands and a bushel of fresh-smelling leaves. He walked past the king, who was waiting at the edge of the forest, making no eye contact.

King Maurice nodded in acknowledgement of Johndor's safe return and in gratitude, knowing the plants were for healing his daughter.

Chapter 3

The king's men continued to search for the mysterious archer, but the forest was dense and the skies darkened almost immediately. A heavy rainstorm broke over the horsemen before they'd made it very far beyond the tree line, making it impossible to see before them. Thunder scared the horses, and they galloped faster than ever back to the castle.

The king now paced nervously by the castle doors, hands tightly gripping his hips. He heard the horses entering the grounds and ran down the steps towards Paul, the lead horseman. Paul shook his head in disappointment. "Nothing, sire. He was too fast, and the storm scared the horses."

"Rainstorm! What rainstorm?" the king shouted as he looked up, stretching his arms toward the clear skies.

"Everyone on guard! Day and night... no one sleeps!" the king shouted, then stormed back into the castle. Bethlynn and Lauren, who were staring out the kitchen window, looked at each other in distress without saying a word, knowing the mood in the castle would be strained. Samuel, who was standing in the front room contemplating all that had happened that day, shook in fear at Maurice's demeanor. Maurice headed up into Princess Isabella's quarters. His anger ceased when he saw Johndor adjusting the strips of linen he'd wrapped over the princess's knees. He stood quietly by the door so as to not disrupt the moment and took a breath of relief to see Isabella was safe. Lilac, who stood on the other side of the bed, stared at Maurice with an angry, blaming look. Minna held a cup of linden tea up for Isabella to sip while Minna recounted the story of how she and Johndor met. Like a favorite book, Isabella could hear it countless times and still become excited over it. Minna edited the story every time to make it funny for Isabella.

"He made me walk miles and miles to meet his family, all while telling me the same story ten times. He promised to carry me when my feet ached from walking, but I was too heavy, and we both fell and rolled down a hill." Minna spun around to demonstrate, inspiring giggles from Isabella.

The king walked in, stood next to Minna, and patted Isabella on the head. He reached down and softly squeezed her nose, bringing more giggles. Looking past his daughter, he saw the bloody rags in Johndor's hands.

King Maurice asked nervously, "How deep did it pierce?"

Johndor angrily ignored the king's question, seeing his erratic behavior as the culprit for the incident. When he finished wrapping Isabella's knees, he answered Maurice while he looked at Isabella. "Not too deep, just an ugly scar at the end."

Maurice looked at Lilac, feeling the heaviness of her gaze, and clenched his jaw in anger at her. Minna, noticing the exchange of hostility, nodded at Johndor, gesturing that they should leave. She kissed Isabella's foot and curtsied as she made her way out with Johndor.

Queen Lilac reached to caress Isabella's head. She suddenly stopped, and her smile slowly faded as her eyes began to water. The queen leapt up, grasped the hem of her sky-blue gown, and rushed out of the room. She ran down the stairs and out the front doors to where she and Isabella had fallen, then dropped to her knees and frantically searched the ground.

The sky darkened and a lightning bolt danced across the gloom. With a loud clash, thunder shook the grounds and rain poured down over Lilac. The king ran out and grabbed Lilac by the arm, yelling over the clattering of the rain and the neighs of the scared horses, "Come inside! Have you lost your mind?"

"My ring!" she replied. "My ring is gone."

King Maurice pulled her up, and she fell against him in utter despair. He grasped her by the shoulders and held her back to inspect her left hand. Her gold and ruby wedding ring was not there. He stared at her bare finger as his anger swelled. He scurried her toward the castle and Minna, who had been discreetly watching from the front door. Lilac fell into Minna's arms, crying like Isabella had earlier.

The front doors slammed. The king jumped on his white horse and galloped off into the forest. The king's horse, Isiah, was not afraid of thunder. His attitude was as strong as his master's. Isiah had been a gift on Maurice's 22nd birthday from his father, and over the years had become a loyal friend and trusted confidante to the king.

Isiah ran as fast as he could through the wet grass and mud. The king didn't know in which direction to guide Isiah, as there was no trace of the archer, but the steed picked a direction, his intuition always keen. Maurice recognized a large oak tree with branches mimicking arms and legs and pulled the reigns to the right as Isiah pulled to the left. The king had never been allowed to explore past that specific oak tree. His parents had told tales of the bewitched and enchanted villagers that lived in that direction. Although they were tales, Maurice had never dared to venture in there until today.

When the king kept pulling the horse to the right, Isiah stopped and began to back up, neighing and swaying his head back and forth and side to side.

"No, Isiah... this way," Maurice yelled as he pulled the reigns with all his might.

Quickly, Isiah took off down the forbidden, narrow path between the strangest of trees. The trees were somehow brighter than any trees Maurice had ever seen. In fact, they seemed to glisten. The muddy, rocky path magically transformed into bright green grass ahead of each step Isiah took. Mesmerized, the king glanced backward, where the path had turned to a rocky, muddy footpath again. Large silver insects flew across his face, but stopped there for a second, as if looking into his eyes.

The king looked around, forgetting the purpose of his journey, awestruck by the enchanted atmosphere. He held his head with his left hand, not sure if he was dizzy or the actual forest was rotating.

Suddenly Isiah halted, then galloped from side to side, confused. The branches of the biggest tree before them parted, and a black crow cackled loudly and soared over the king and his horse. The king followed the crow with his eyes, wide-eyed and open-mouthed to witness such shiny wings. In fact, he could swear they were lined in silver. Isiah followed the crow with a mesmerized rhythm, straight into a thick forest of more odd-looking trees. Some were tall and thin. Others were as wide as a small house, with different trunks winding around each other, decorating each other with a myriad of different leaves, as if they were a family of different breeds birthing from the one very thick, black root.

The crow disappeared from their sight in the thickness of the trees above.

The king feared they were lost and wanted to turn back, but he did not know which way was back any more. He swore he heard a woman's voice calling in a soft and slow tone on the wind. Maurice directed Isiah towards the sultry voice.

Confused and taken aback, the king's goal of capturing the archer had become second to his urge to discover more about this mysterious place they had stumbled upon. Isiah followed the king's gaze, turning circles three times in slow motion. Somehow the trees seem to have changed from shiny bright leaves to a darker olive color. And neither the king nor his loyal steed could tell any longer which direction they'd just been facing.

Raindrops began to trickle down, and the king thought perhaps it was the rain that had changed the color of the leaves. He looked up as his surroundings grew dimmer and he noticed a large gray cloud moving closer to them. Noticing that Isiah was paralyzed and staring at the cloud, he pulled the reigns and pushed hard on the saddle, ordering Isiah to move. A startled Isiah leaned back on his hind legs and galloped forward, not knowing where he was headed, but trying to get away from the growing gray cloud that seemed to be following them.

The forest became denser and denser with trees the farther they went. In shock, the king had Isiah cut through the thickness of the forestry. He took his gaze away from the cloud and looked forward. He rubbed his eyes in disbelief, seeing that the trees appeared to be magically moving out of Isiah's path.

A heavy, vibrating clash of thunder unlike the king or Isiah had ever heard before scared the horse to a screeching halt, sending Maurice jolting forward.

Hot, heavy raindrops came down stronger and stronger, obstructing Isiah's view. He quickly moved under a large mushroom-shaped tree nearby with hundreds of thin branches hanging over the ground like an umbrella. This most peculiar tree dangled hundreds of odd, jagged leaves that each looked like two thunderbolts facing each other. The leaves' color changed from green to violet and back to green so that just when the eye was sure the leaf was green, it became violet, and then, certain that it was violet, it became green again.

Exhausted and relieved to have cover from the violent downpour,

Isiah, forcing Maurice off his back with a shake of his body, slowly lay down to rest as Maurice sat next to him on the wet ground. A half hour passed before the rain settled slowly. Maurice dared to pull a leaf from the mushroom-shaped tree. As he rubbed the leaf between his fingers to decipher its color and velvety texture, the leaf turned to ashes. A strong gust of wind brought a whiff of sulfur and separated the branches, opening a view for Isiah and the king.

Maurice stared in surprise as a small thatched house came into view. He straightened his back in disbelief. Isiah stood up quickly. They both stood frozen, staring at this gray and black cottage in the middle of a mysterious nowhere. The chase for the archer had been completely dismissed. Intrigue had set in.

Maurice grabbed Isiah's reigns and walked him towards the cottage under gentle pellets of rain. He sensed a somewhat dark nature as he noticed that adorning two small windows, there seemed to be the remains of bushels of flowers either missing their buds or already withered. The strong, sharp smell of sulfur in the air made Isiah shake his head from side to side and stop moving forward. Maurice pulled a silk cloth from his pocket and covered his nose. Staring at the windows, he was certain he saw shadows moving inside the cottage although he was still yards away.

With a loud clash of thunder, another heavy downpour broke, settling the smell of the sulfur, but sending Isiah running for shelter, right to the front of the cottage, with Maurice running quickly behind.

The rain stopped in an instant. A haggard old woman stood outside the front door holding some rags. She turned to whisper quick, stern words through the slightly open front door, then turned back and smiled at Maurice. She held up her hand to Isiah's mouth and offered what looked like sugar cubes. Isiah neighed as she reached and put them into his mouth. She opened the thick rags in her hands, releasing the sweet smell of cinnamon, and offered them to Maurice. The rags were warm and dry, so Maurice placed one around his shoulders and back, and the other over Isiah's back. Isiah's legs weakened and shook a little as he slowly settled under the roof and gently fell asleep.

The old lady opened the door widely, ushering Maurice inside.

Chapter 4

The mood in the castle was quiet and tense. Queen Lilac was lying sprawled on the floor of her quarters, crying over the loss of her ring, a symbol that meant so much to her.

The princess played in her bedroom with her favorite toy. Johndor had crafted the wooden horse for her as a birthday gift, and she'd named it Rose at Johndor's suggestion, since the wood had been sanded to a rose tone. Minna watched Isabella as she dusted the curtain panels, looking out the window every now and then for any signs of the king's return. She stared for a minute at dark clouds nearing the grounds until she felt a pull on her skirt. She looked down at Isabella, who was in search of her attention, then squatted down and hugged the child.

Isabella whimpered, "I want my father."

"He shall return soon, my darling," Minna said gently, smoothing Isabella's long hair with her hand.

Isabella moved around nervously and cried louder, "I want my father to come back right now!"

Queen Lilac heard the cries and pulled herself up to the burgundy satin Bordeaux covers of her bed. She climbed on the bed and dropped herself down, face first, unable to deal with Isabella when she could hardly come to her own wits. She stretched across the bed and pounded the mattress with her fists.

Minna picked Isabella up and lay with her on her bed and told her a story about when she was a little girl and her mother had given her a doll she called Penelope. When Minna lost Penelope, she'd cried incessantly. Her mother told her about how Penelope had gone off to do something important and would come back when she was ready, and every tear cried would make her take longer. Isabella cried herself to sleep as Minna told the story, her little body jolting from time to time. Minna stared off into the distance, remembering how she found Penelope when she had been packing her things on her wedding day, inside a large tapestry bag. She smiled and dozed off with Isabella in her arms.

DING! DING! The six o'clock evening bells rang throughout the castle. It had been nothing less than a dim, somber day.

Queen Lilac, who had also fallen into a hapless slumber, awoke to realize that King Maurice had not returned. She ran down the corridor opening every door, looking for him. "Maurice! Maurice!" she called out as she rushed down the stairs and into the kitchen.

Maidens Bethlynn and Lauren looked up from washing dishes as Lilac ran past with a disturbed look on her face.

"Hasn't returned," Bethlynn said stoically, returning to her duty.

Caught by Queen Lilac's gaze, Lauren stared back, grasping her apron nervously and shaking her head no.

Lilac ran to the castle doors and pushed them open, fixing her right shoe, which had fallen off from her aimless running. She saw Johndor making his way back from the stable where he had secured the horses. She ran to him and held his shoulders, yelling, "Johndor, Johndor... where is he? Has he returned?"

"No, my lady... I'm afraid not."

He looked up to the sky and took a deep, worry-filled breath at the thought of night about to fall upon them. Though the king had enjoyed a handful of disappearing acts before, Johndor knew this was different.

Chapter 5

A small flock of peculiar, tiny birds resembling hummingbirds glittered in metallic peachy colors as they fluttered their shiny wings close to Isiah's face as he lay in deep slumber. The birds' trumpet-shaped beaks screeched a high-pitched tone in an orchestrated manner. They fluttered their wings so fast, it looked as if shining stars were raining glitter over Isiah. He continued in his deep repose, snoring, his lips vibrating, then falling closed with a plopping sound.

Inside the thatched cottage, King Maurice sat in a large, rounded armchair. The purple velvet seat was thick and cushioned his backside, which was sore from riding. He stared at the rags warming strategically by the fireplace, as if waiting for a guest.

The old lady crouched on a black footstool between the fireplace and King Maurice. Just before her bottom touched the seat of the footstool, she tossed a small item into the fireplace, causing the flames to spark up. Maurice glanced immediately at her hands, but they were empty. Her long, bony, crooked fingers reached toward his boots.

He pulled his feet back. "That's not necessary," he said uncomfortably, yet gently, trying not to insult the old lady who had offered him and his steed such hospitality. She let out a sharp laugh, almost like the cackling of a crow, leaned to her left, and yelled into the kitchen. "Bring it now!"

A glass shattered.

The old lady flared her nostrils as she rose quickly. Dragging her right leg, she bustled to the kitchen. Maurice turned to look as he heard the voice of a distressed younger woman. "I'm sorry, Nan Marguarite. I'm—"

"Give me here!" the old lady said sternly, snatching a small amber bottle from the young woman's grip.

The woman pled, "No, wait, Nan, hold on, I've already—"

"Watch and learn, Maggy Mae," the old lady said. She tipped the amber bottle slowly until three thick drops poured into the hot cup of tea the younger woman had been preparing. Light smoke scattered and twisted upward like a tiny tornado.

"Smell it! Smell it! Quickly!" she whispered softly yet firmly to Maggy Mae as to assure Maurice wouldn't hear, then chanted, "The leaves we will take as the branches weave, we will boil, he will drink, he will never leave."

Maggy Mae bent over and inhaled slowly as the smoke twisted faster and faster, entering both her nostrils, then took a step back and covered her tearing eyes.

"It will pass," the old lady said, followed by her cackling laugh. She gently shoved Maggy Mae by her waist toward the sitting area. "Let's go now."

Maurice tried to make sense of what he'd heard coming from the kitchen. He tried to focus on the muffled sound of voices on the other side of the wall behind him. He was not sure which he was more confused about: their mysterious chattering or the old lady's accent, which sounded like a blend of French and Scottish.

He heard the women's footsteps coming from kitchen and turned to look. Grinning, the old lady gave the younger woman a slight nudge, moving her next to Maurice. He was surprised at the sight of the flustered young woman offering him a cup of tea but accepted the cup and saucer with a small nod of thanks. Both ladies stood tense until he took the first taste.

Marguarite let out a sigh of relief and unclenched her hands, letting them relax by her sides.

Maurice watched Maggy Mae as she brushed her black, wavy hair away from her face, exposing her dark black eyes. Her upturned nose reminded him of a piglet's snout.

Marguarite grasped the young woman by both shoulders and pressed her forward as she said, "This is my granddaughter, Maggy Mae."

When Maggy Mae extended a trembling hand to shake Maurice's, the corner of her wide orange sleeve tipped the teacup, spilling some tea onto the saucer. Marguarite grabbed the teacup from Maurice and walked quickly into the kitchen, her right leg dragging behind her hurried body. Her wrinkly, crooked fingers shook in anger as she poured more tea to refill the cup, grabbed the small amber bottle of potion, and poured three more drops.

"Maggy!" she yelled, moving toward the sitting room again.

Maggy tripped over the black footstool, recovering quickly to meet Marguarite halfway as she walked out of the kitchen.

"Smell it! Smell it!" Marguarite whispered as the smoke twisted in an upward spiral.

"No, Nan—" Maggy begged, pushing away the cup her grandmother was forcing on her.

"Smell it, girl! You want to be rich? You want to be queen?"

Maggy grimaced and tipped her head, but a draft came through the cracked window and broke up the spiraling smoke. She covered her mouth in fear of Marguarite's reaction, then sighed in relief when she saw her grandmother looking at Maurice, as he had stood up to check on Isiah. Marguarite began to tremble with anguish, afraid the king might escape before she had time to bewitch him. She pushed Maggy out of the way, handing her the teacup, and scurried to Maurice.

"Sit down. You must drink this tea so the wet winds will not sicken your bones." She laughed a nervous, yet evil, laugh. "Listen to the old lady... she knows best," she said, patting his arm. "Sit... sit."

Maurice sat with a confused look on his face, frustrated at the fact that he had lost power over his own will.

"Bring him the tea, Maggy!" Marguarite yelled assertively, with a smile on her face, not losing sight of Maurice. As Maggy approached, the old woman reached for the cup. With a quick hand, she grabbed a hair from Maggy's curl and dropped it in the tea, then snatched the cup and saucer from the girl and handed it to Maurice. He held the teacup, sat back comfortably in the velvet chair, and drank.

"Thank you, Madam Marguarite," he said, giving his head a firm bow.

A thumping and scratching sound startled Maurice, making him reach to set his cup down on the mirrored table next to the chair.

Marguarite quickly pushed the cup back toward him. "I will check your steed," she said. "Maggy! Dry his boots!"

The old lady reached into the pocket of her lacy black cotton dress as she opened the front door. Isiah had thumped his hoofs on the wooden planks while trying to shoo away the birds. Marguarite stepped out and closed the door behind her. The trumpeting humming of the peculiar birds rose to a higher pitch. Flapping their miniscule shiny wings, the birds flew away at the speed of light and disappeared into the sky.

Marguarite carefully stooped over Isiah, bending her left knee slowly. "Now, now, sleep, horse, sleep." She pressed three white squares into Isiah's open mouth and tried to push his stretched-out leg down.

Standing slowly while leaning on the window for support, she moved quietly to take a peek inside through the window. The white squares had worked quickly, and Isiah had slipped into a trance-like sleep, making his leg drop like a heavy brick. At that precise moment,

Marguarite tried to cross over him to get a closer look in the window and in doing so, tripped over his leg. She tried to catch her fall, but her lacy dress caught on a nail sticking out of a board, her foot caught under Isiah's leg, and she hit the ground head first, making the last thumping sound to be heard for a while.

Isiah's senses were numbed so profoundly that he was not aware of the fallen old lady. Maggy Mae and Maurice, trusting Marguarite was checking on the thumping noises, paid no mind. The old lady's bony fingers reached toward the door as if to call for help. Her hand dropped, her breathing stopped, her eyes became fixed open. A stream of blood slid across the wooden planks of the front porch. Nan Marguarite was dead.

Thick, hot drops of rain began to fall slowly over the perimeter of the grounds. Quickly, the rain began to pour more forcefully, and a bright glare could be seen rising up from behind the trees in the far eastward direction.

Chapter 6

Back at the castle at half past six in the evening, the king's men gathered in the great hall to discuss the absence of His Majesty.

The lead horseman, Paul, stood in front to address the other men. "We shall wait one more hour. If he has not returned by then, we will take it upon ourselves to begin a search before the dark of night falls."

Although Johndor was not part of the king's men, he sat in. As everyone well knew, Johndor was the king's best advisor and a father figure to him. Johndor nodded once in agreement and walked away, head down, squinting his eyebrows and clicking his tongue in disbelief.

Exhausted from the day's troubles, Minna slept on, dreaming of her mother and her doll Penelope and smiling at the pleasant dream. The doors of the princess's quarters flew open and Queen Lilac burst in, not realizing both Minna and Isabella were deep in sleep.

The princess jerked, and Minna startled up halfway, protectively cradling Isabella.

"You must help me, Minna. I know you can. I have heard tales about your sister, Thumbeline," Lilac begged.

"Momma, Momma!" the princess cried, reaching for her mother.

Lilac tried to lay her back down. "Go back to sleep, darling. Minna and I need to speak."

Lilac yelled, "Lauren! Bethlynn!" as she pulled frantically at Minna to get her out of Isabella's bed.

"Please, Your Majesty!" Minna said assertively. "I can get up by myself!" Minna dusted off her apron and corrected the white coronet lace-edged cap on her head. "Now, what is happening?"

The queen ushered her out the door, whispering under her breath so as not to allow Lauren and Bethlynn to hear. "He hasn't returned. Maurice hasn't returned, and night is upon us. I have a terrible feeling, Minna."

Minna walked toward the door. "I will go straight away to the chapel and—"

"To the chapel?" questioned Lilac in a loud whisper. "I know about your sister, Minna. Please tell me where she is. We must find her right away."

Minna turned around. "I suggest we do some praying before jumping to conclusions."

"The arrow, the ring, and Maurice missing. Something is terribly wrong. I'm certain that arrow was cursed, Minna. There is no time to waste. Take me to her at once!" demanded the queen.

Minna took a deep breath, seeing the pain in the queen's eyes. "Yes, Your Majesty. I will order Samuel to prepare the coach."

Minna made her way downstairs and waited outside the great hall for Johndor and Samuel to exit the gathering with the king's men so she could inform the two men of Lilac's orders.

The king's men prepared horses for the search. The five horses and their men were geared up and ready to go when a coach pulled up behind them. Puzzled, the men looked at each other, wondering at who had given that command.

Cloaked for the chilly evening, the queen and Minna rushed out of the castle and stepped into the coach. Close on their heels, Johndor climbed inside the coach as well. The queen was surprised at his forward gesture. Minna, on the other hand, was relieved.

The queen's coach set out in a northward direction. Paul yelled out and the five king's men headed west into the dark forest, fire sconces in hand, kicking up a cloud of dirt behind them.

Chapter 7

Back in the cottage in the mysterious land, King Maurice sat sipping the tea and warming by the fire as Maggy Mae hovered nearby, hands clutched in front of her. She stared in awe that the king so many sought was sitting in her abode. And if the spell worked as her Nan promised, he would soon be hers.

Feeling uncomfortable with the silence, Maurice said, "That's quite a storm. Does it usually rain so much out... here?" trying to think of the name of the region.

Maggy Mae shook her head nervously. "It doesn't ever. No, not this hard." She waited for him to take another sip of tea. "Have you never been over this way? To Nokbershire?"

Looking at the window to his left and trying to get a peek through a slit in the heavy olive-green curtains, Maurice squinted for any sign of Isiah. "I haven't had the pleasure of traveling through these grounds," he said distractedly. He was growing more and more concerned that the thumping had stopped and Nan Marguarite had not come back in the house.

The rain soon flooded the front porch, followed by a bolt of lightning that illuminated the sky, startling Isiah. The hair of the old hag lying across him lit up in electrified streaks as the lightning channeled through the metal residue she had accumulated in her hair. Isiah neighed loudly in fear as a loud, rumbling thunder vibrated the grounds. He jumped up, but he couldn't quite straighten his trembling hind legs and so he struggled to stay upright on just his forelegs. Through his blurry vision, he could see a black shape drifting away from him.

King Maurice set his teacup down and jumped from his chair when he heard Isiah neigh fearfully. He ran to the door and tried to push it open, but cold, murky water began rushing into the house as the door opened.

Maggy Mae yelped, pushed past the king, and quickly shut the door.

Maurice stared at her in disbelief at her unexpected, aggressive action. *Does she not care about the old hag?* he thought. "I must tend to my steed!" he said firmly.

She leaned against the door with her arms wide open and said, "The house will flood if you open the door!"

He stepped over to the window and pulled one curtain panel aside, then called out, "Isiah!" while tapping on the window. Isiah straightened his hind legs and turned to the window, neighing gently three times.

The rain hitting the window impeded Maurice's view, but he was satisfied with Isiah's calmer neighs. Maurice paced around the small house, looking out all the windows for any sign of the old lady or any means of escape. His large boots on the wet floor caused a thumping, squeaking harmony.

Just a few feet away, the corpse of old Nan Marguarite floated farther away until it fell into a trench near the forest entrance. Gobs of mud lifted by the pelting rain covered her lifeless body until she was buried in the trench.

Maggy Mae stood frozen in front of the door, following Maurice with her eyes.

He looked out the front window to check on Isiah again. The rain had dwindled quite a bit, so he was able to see the blurry, large white figure of the horse on the front porch. He sighed in relief at knowing Isiah was okay. He looked straight ahead to the two strange trees with branches meeting at the top and forming a braided structure. He recognized it as the spot they had entered through and therefore, as the way out. Underneath it, a pool of black mud that resembled quicksand caught his eye, its slow motion making it appear alive.

King Maurice gazed up at the quickly darkening sky, wondering where the time had gone. He stood looking out the window in deep thought. Something is not right here, and I must get past this girl. I'll push the door open, jump on Isiah and head out through the peculiar trees. With a confident deep breath, he started to turn toward the door, but movement at the corner of his eye caught his attention. Isiah lay down slowly and fell into yet another slumber.

"Isiah!" Maurice shouted, knocking on the window.

Isiah let out a weak snore.

"No, Isiah, I beg you," he whispered under his breath.

His relentless desire to leave was palpable to Maggy Mae. Growing desperate and nervous, she ran to the window and called out for Nan Marguarite, the only one she thought could convince the king to stay.

Seeing no sign of her grandmother, Maggy Mae rushed out the door and slammed it shut, then held it with all her strength while she yelled for Nan.

The loud slam of the door scared Isiah into more frightened neighing, and he lurched about until he managed to stand up.

Maurice heard Isiah and laughed in great satisfaction as he forced the door open, sending Maggy Mae to the ground. He quickly straddled Isiah, but the horse's knees buckled from the weight. Maurice sat with his legs stretched on the ground on either side of his loyal steed, frozen with surprise.

Maggy Mae rushed to Isiah and held his face, looking up at Maurice tenderly. "Please don't go, please!" she begged. "He's leaving, Nan!" she shouted with all her might.

A fierce draft knocked a silver bowl sitting on the inside window sill into the glass pane, startling Maggy Mae. She dashed inside, yelling, "Nan? Nan, was that you?"

Maurice pulled hard on Isiah's reigns. Isiah struggled to his feet and rode away from the house, toward the edge of the forest where the two tall trees marked the entrance... precisely where the earth had swallowed the old hag.

Chapter 8

Isabella sat on the floor by her bedroom window daydreaming as she stared at the moonlight dancing in her gaze. Bethlynn took hold of Isabella's hands, which were interlaced under her chin, and pulled her up from the floor.

"Wonder what Her Majesty is up to now?" asked Lauren as she placed the tray on Isabella's tea table.

Bethlynn replied to Lauren as she propped herself up on Isabella's bed, sitting the exhausted princess on her lap. "Up to no good, I assure you. You know how she is; must always have her way."

"Tea?" asked Lauren in a gleeful tone.

"Tea indeed," Bethlynn answered with a stern nod.

Bethlynn rocked the golden-haired princess on her lap until she fell asleep, then gently laid her on the bed, and made her way to Isabella's tea table in the far corner of the room to join Lauren.

Lauren plopped the sugar cubes into the teacups.

"Extra sugar?" Bethlynn asked.

"But of course," Lauren replied.

"Dee-lightful." Bethlynn brought the teacup to her thin pink lips.

The ladies sat chatting nonsense about the queen and her over-exaggerated reactions.

"She should have known better," Lauren stated.

"He is a sly fox, that one," Bethlynn replied.

"I overheard her tell Minna she was certain the arrow was cursed," Lauren whispered, cupping her hand over the side of her mouth.

The nonsense chattering and gossiping continued for hours.

Chapter 9

The coach traveled northward two hours, heading towards Minna's sister Thumbeline's house in South Cuvington, with the impatient queen holding on to Minna's hand and staring out the window piercingly, as if looking for any sign of the king. Johndor took a long, slow whiff, raising his head slowly as he closed his eyes. Minna smiled slightly.

"We are close," Johndor said.

"Gardenias?" Minna asked.

Johndor nodded firmly, then turned to open the velvet curtain behind him and shouted at Samuel. "Veer right at the next oak tree and follow the stone path."

"Sir," Samuel acknowledged.

The queen held Minna's hand tighter and fixed a fearful, wide-eyed gaze on the exhausted matron. Minna smiled and gave her queen's hand a gentle squeeze, but her smile couldn't hide her worry over the missing king.

Far in the distance, a light appeared. Johndor ordered Samuel to steer the carriage toward the light that was coming from Thumbeline's house. Four more lights turned on in a row beyond the first, one at a time, allowing a most peculiar wooden house, perfectly entrenched between the trees, to come into view ahead of them. The coach stopped, and Johndor jumped off and walked toward a gardenia bush. He snapped off a gardenia and returned to help Minna out of the coach, then handed her the fragile bud. She held it to her nose and smelled deeply, allowing her eyes to close gently as she took in the essence of the soft white flower.

"I will take it to Isabella," she said, tucking the stem into her brassiere.

Samuel helped Queen Lilac out and walked with her to the small wooden house. Samuel and Lilac stared in awe at what seemed to be a house perfectly built by branches of uniting trees.

Minna stood next to Samuel and Lilac and began to explain the bizarre formation. "Many years ago, during a bad storm, the trees magically moved and bent to protect the house and those inside it. It's been as such ever since."

A creak drew their attention to the front door just as it slowly opened. They couldn't see anyone, but heard, "Please, please, come in already. You don't want the bugs to get in, now do you?"

The queen stepped in carefully, watching her step and holding up her dress so as not to let it drag. Minna and Johndor followed the queen inside, shutting the door behind them. Lilac scrunched her nose at the sudden smell of burning grass as she looked around for the person whose voice she'd heard.

A wrinkly old lady sat in a rocking chair with two big wheels on its side that moved, seemingly on its own, toward the group. The thick, red velvet cushion she sat on was covered with small burn holes. Her copper hair was held tight to the top center of her head, with gold ribbons covering the entire bun and a white crocheted wool shawl around her shoulders. The old lady held a pipe tight between her lips and her gaze fixed on Lilac as her chair slowly crossed the front room.

Lilac took a step back, pressing against the front door. The old lady grasped the pipe with her left hand and reached her right hand out to the queen. She flashed a big smile with her tongue between her toothless gums.

Feeling a little confused by the old lady's assertive yet sweet, loving smile, Lilac reached her hand out.

Shaking hands with the queen, the old lady said, "I am Thumbeline." Then she bowed her head in the proper greeting of royalty.

"Queen Lilac," she replied with a slight curtsy.

Thumbeline burst out in laughter. "A queen in my tree house," she said softly, exploring every inch of Lilac's hand.

"Please sit, my queen, as I boil some water for tea," Thumbline went on, as Lilac made her way with Minna and Johndor to the front room and sat on a mint-colored silk settee with Johndor. Minna sat on her father's old chair, smiling proudly.

"Where did the nobleman go?" Thumbeline asked.

Johndor replied, "Samuel waits in the coach, as this visit should be a quick one."

"A quick one. Ha!" Thumbeline replied. "He shouldn't have to wait in the cold night—not to mention the bugs. Bring him in. The tea is on." She pointed her pipe at Johndor as she spoke.

Thumbeline looked at Minna, who sat in their father's old chair, and her smile loosened a little.

"My sister, you look pale. I shall fix you a special tea." She looked at Johndor with melancholic eyes. Minna's pale face and level of animation reminded her of when their mother became ill. Thumbeline requested that Johndor bring her leaves for a blood tea. "And don't forget to ask the bush for permission! Make sure the nobleman also has tea!" She looked at the queen and, pointing with her pipe toward a room at the back of the house, said, "Can I get a little push, please?"

"Of course," Lilac replied as she stood up. She looked at Minna, asking with her eyes for her to accompany them.

Cackling loudly, Thumbeline said, "Well, the wheels on this chair aren't going to roll themselves, now."

Minna gave a gentle hand gesture, letting Lilac know she would be fine without her.

"I will not bite, I promise. I have no teeth. Ha ha!" Thumbeline said.

Johndor and Samuel stepped inside and gently closed the door behind them. Johndor headed to the kitchen to tend to the tea as Samuel joined Minna in the front room and asked respectfully if he might have a whiff of the white gardenia. Minna gave Samuel a gentle look, then pulled the flower out of her brassiere and held it to his nose as he inhaled deeply.

Thumbeline reached forward to grab the doorknob, although the door was still a few feet away. Lilac looked all around, still trying to figure out if Thumbeline had legs under the thick, golden-poppy-colored blanket on her lap. Thumbeline's fingers finally touched the doorknob and she opened the door. Lilac pushed the wheelchair into the room, at first surprised by the many candles outlining all four walls of the small room.

"Shut the door please," Thumbeline said in a serious tone.

"Oh yes, the bugs," Lilac replied.

"There are no bugs inside the house," Thumbeline replied with a bit of sarcasm.

"Of course not," Lilac said sheepishly. She turned and closed the door quietly. As she turned back to push Thumbeline across the room, she found her already on the other side of the room, sitting behind a long rectangular table covered in a variety of colored tapestries.

Thumbeline pointed to a small, square, wooden stool-like seat with a round, golden- colored cushion. "Sit."

Lilac quickly walked over and sat down facing Thumbeline across the table.

"What brings you here to my humble abode?" Thumbeline asked.

"Well, a mystery man shot an arrow. I'm sure it was cursed, and it hit—"

"I know why you're here." Thumbeline pursed her lips around her pipe and stared at a glass of water. "I see a curse, and I see something is missing... something is lost."

"Yes, my wedding ring is lost," Lilac said, her voice breaking. Thumbeline shook her head slowly side to side.

Lilac blurted out, "And that arrow was cursed, and it broke my daughter's skin... now I'm afraid she is cursed." She began to sob. "And my husband has left to find this mystery archer, but not returned. I fear he may be captured. I fear he may be... dead." She covered her face with her hands and fell into wracking sobs.

"The king... dead?" Thumbeline said, looking again into the glass of water, seeing an apparition of a smoky figure of a man on a horse ever so briefly that quickly dispersed back into the water.

"He is not dead, but this curse cannot be reversed. Although all will be well." She quickly dumped the glass of water into a brass bowl. "I am sorry," she said, looking up at Lilac. With a smile, she said sweetly, "Can you please give me a push?"

Lilac stood frozen in shock by Thumbeline's findings, then dropped to her knees and clutched her hands together in prayer to her host. "Please, remove the curse, please!"

Lilac's head fell onto Thumbeline's hands, which were folded on her lap. Thumbeline pulled one hand up and placed it over Lilac's head and whispered some words in prayer. She gently pulled Lilac's head up.

"I do not possess that kind of power. Time has the winning hand this time," she said, wheeling herself out of the room and leaving Lilac on her knees in the prayer room. Thumbeline placed herself next to Minna. She held Minna's hands in hers and said,

"Please come back soon. We are getting wiser, if you know what I mean. Soon we will be part of the celestial sky."

Lilac stood up and walked out of the prayer room slowly and stood in front of Thumbeline. As Lilac was about to speak, Thumbeline said, gently reaching for her hands, "Pray. Pray a lot. For the princess, for the king, and for yourself." She kissed the queen's hands and released them.

Minna put down the blood tea Johndor had made for her as she stood and discreetly placed a few gold coins in her sister's hand. Thumbeline flashed her a big smile. "Now leave quickly. You do not want to get caught out there in the midnight hour."

Johndor chuckled at Thumbeline's superstitious beliefs, although he respected them altogether. "Let's move quickly," he said.

"I hope you enjoyed your tea, Samuel," Thumbeline said, giving his hand a squeeze of good luck as he made his way out the door with Lilac, Johndor, and Minna. Johndor and Minna walked quickly to the coach, as Samuel and Lilac stepped backwards carefully, admiring the exterior of the house.

They stepped into the coach and started on their way back to the castle. As they approached the oak tree, they noticed an old hag walking in the distance. Closer still, Johndor and Minna recognized the short, pudgy woman wearing a gray wool hat and gloves as Thumbeline's nosy and spiteful neighbor Carmile.

Johndor shouted at Samuel when he realized the carriage was slowing down. "Keep going. Keep going!"

Carmile stopped and turned back toward her house. "Royalty... hmm," she said to herself, rubbing her hands and fingers together as if conjuring up an evil scheme.

As Carmile watched the coach disappear into the night, she approached Thumbeline regarding the night's royal visit. Thumbeline made it clear to Carmile that the reason for the visit was a curse without resolve and assured her that all her Germanic witchery and sorcery would never be enough.

Carmile saw this as an opportunity to gain riches from the queen's desperation. Thumbeline was never rude to anyone, even to Carmile, as Carmile's daughter had been widowed by Thumbeline's son, and they shared two lovely granddaughters, whom became estranged after a mosquito carrying an irreversible disease claimed the life of Thumbeline's son.

Chapter 10

Maurice urged Isiah forward, but the steed bucked and kicked his front legs out when they got close to the forest's edge. Nearly falling off, Maurice yelled, "Isiah, settle down, boy! It's getting darker; we must go!"

Isiah jumped around and kicked his legs over the site where the earth had swallowed Nan Marguarite. A large thunderbolt cracked in the sky and lightning illuminated the evening for a mere second. A heavy downpour began to fall.

Maurice tried to persuade Isiah to cross into the forest with rein and whip, but the horse refused, and instead ran laps around the cottage as if in a race.

Afraid and holding on tighter, Maurice could not get him to stop. He wrapped the black leather straps around his hands and leaned into Isiah, whispering in his ear, "It's okay, boy. It's okay. Settle down now. It's okay."

Isiah slowed down, and Maurice patted his head gently. The rain poured down harder. Maurice was forced to direct Isiah back to the cottage's front porch for shelter from the thick, pelting raindrops.

Maggy Mae saw their shadows through the window and opened the door with a confused look. She was happy to see the king, but upset Nan had not come back. "Is he alright?" she asked, seeing by his shaking and teeth gnashing that Isiah was clearly agitated.

Maurice saw the white cubes the old hag had fed Isiah in the silver bowl on the window ledge. He grabbed some to reward Isiah for settling down.

Maggy Mae reached to stop him, but then quickly stepped back.

Maurice held the cubes out to Isiah with one hand and patted his head with the other. Isiah eagerly ate up all the sugar cubes, and just as quickly dropped to the floor. He took one big breath, and no more followed.

Maurice fell to his knees and shook his noble steed's head, calling out, "Isiah! Isiah!"

Isiah's eyes were half open. Maurice reached to feel for Isiah's heart, finding only stiffness and cold settling in. No warmth, no beating heart.

Maurice's heart sank in sadness. He held up his arms, and with raging anger, released a loud outcry to the heavens. He fell over Isiah in a heap of confusion and anger and cried for a half a minute. He stood up and wiped his tears, not wanting Maggy Mae to see his weakness. He turned and stared at the timid young woman.

Maggy Mae shivered and took a step back from the look of anger on Maurice's face. A tear fell to her cheek as she said, "Nan is gone, isn't she?"

Maurice nodded his head in agreement, though he didn't really know what had happened to the old woman. He walked past Maggy Mae and entered the cottage, becoming more emotionless with every step and feeling as if he were having a nightmare.

Maggy Mae ran in after him and fell to her knees weeping, face in her hands. She reached out and offered Maurice a piece of Nan's dress that she had just found on a nail sticking up from the porch. She continued to cry, sobbing loudly, bent double.

Maurice's heart softened at seeing Maggy Mae in such anguish. He lifted her shaking body and cradled her in his arms, then hugged her tightly with his own need for solace as well. She wrapped her arms around his strong back.

Patting her wavy black hair, Maurice soothed, "Here, here, it's alright now." He kissed the crown of her head and rocked her gently like a child as her body shook with sobs.

Her crying dwindled gradually, but she kept her head on his chest and her arms wrapped around his body. Then she reached for the back of his head and pulled him down as she reached her lips to meet his. Mystified, Maurice somehow found himself allowing her to do so. His hopeless romantic needs and the bewitched tea led Maurice to bed Maggy Mae that night.

Chapter 11

The sunshine of a new day shone through the stained-glass windows of Queen Lilac's quarters. She sat up in the bed quickly, angry that exhaustion had gotten the best of her and she'd fallen asleep.

"Minna!" she yelled.

She was about to call out again, but she heard the clicking of Minna's shoes down the hall. Queen Lilac kicked off the gilded Bordeaux covers trapping her in the bed and ran to the window to search for any signs that the king might have returned.

A gentle knock on the door, followed by a weak voice, interrupted the queen's search. "Minna here."

"Come, come, Minna," Lilac said.

Minna entered, with a very dim look to her otherwise bright eyes.

"Is he here?" Lilac asked in excitement. "Did he arrive while I was asleep?"

"I'm afraid not, Your Majesty. Sir Paul left word about another search during daylight. Perhaps they will be successful on this go."

"Minna, your sister Thumbeline said she saw a curse and a loss but no death. Perhaps he is just lost in the woods. Maybe Isiah ran off."

Minna slid the curtains apart as she spoke. "Perhaps, perhaps.

We shall keep praying."

Lilac scurried to Minna and grasped her cold hands. "Your sister said she could not remove the curse. I am worried about the princess. It is my fault. That arrow should have hit me, not her. We will always have to watch her carefully. She should not ever leave this castle."

Minna turned away to stare at the blue unicorn tapestry hanging over the queen's bed. In disbelief, she said over her shoulder, "I will make Lauren and Bethlynn aware of your instructions, but I think—"

A gentle knock on the door interrupted Minna and Lilac.

"Please enter," Lilac said as she gestured for Minna to help her don her sky-blue satin dress.

"Pardon," Lauren said. "There is an old lady wishing to have a word with Queen Lilac. Looked familiar."

Bethlynn popped her head in behind Lauren, startling Lauren. Lauren yelped, then covered her mouth and giggled. Bethlynn said, "It's Carmile, Minna. Shall I see that old witch out?"

Lauren's smile turned to an open circle and her eyes widened.

"Witch?" Lilac said in a surprised tone. "No! See her in. I will see her in the study."

"As you wish, Lilac... Queen," Bethlynn said cuttingly, as she turned and walked away.

Lauren scurried behind Bethlynn, whispering, "Bethy Bethy... what's happening?"

Minna stepped in front of Lilac to stop her from walking out the door. "Lilac, Johndor and I would both advise against meeting with Carmile. She is full of piecrust promises—easily made, easily broken. She is known for her gold-digging ways."

"But, Minna, she may have news about Maurice's whereabouts," Lilac replied as she gently moved Minna out of her way and hurried down to the study.

Minna walked fast, trying to keep up with Lilac. When they passed Lauren, Minna turned and said, "The princess is to be kept inside at all times."

Princess Isabella heard her mother walking past and rushed to the door, leaving Bethlynn holding the strands of her golden hair that she'd been trying to brush. "Momma, Momma," she shouted, running to her mother and grabbing her around the hips. "Bethlynn made my head hurt."

Lilac tried to release Isabella's strong grip, sounding annoyed as she said, "Not now, darling. We've got to find your father."

Minna picked Isabella up, breaking her grip on her mother's skirt. "I have a gift for you. Let Bethlynn finish brushing your hair, and I will bring it to you. Go on now," Minna said, scooting her back inside her quarters. Minna whispered to Bethlynn, "She is not to go outside."

Isabella walked back in skipping, holding her arms around her head. She jumped up and down in excitement. "What is it? What is my gift?"

Bethlynn began to recite a rhyme. "Perhaps it's an ox or a box—"

Lauren joined in. "... or a fox."

"A fox?" squealed the princess.

The three laughed and danced around the room as they continued the guessing game. Minna slipped out to resume following the queen.

Lilac tread quickly down the stairs, reaching the bottom, where she saw Johndor speaking with Carmile at the front door. Lilac slowly made her way to Johndor.

Upon seeing Johndor intervening with Carmile when she approached the bottom of the stairs, Minna was relieved, knowing he always meant business and that no one could swindle him. She made her way into the kitchen and picked up the small vase with the white gardenia flower Johndor had snapped from Thumbeline's front yard. In Minna's family, it was tradition that when a white gardenia gets passed on, so do the blessings of the ancestors. Minna was proud to gift the flower to Isabella. She enjoyed the flower's sweet, heady scent as she made her way back upstairs.

Johndor continued to question Carmile about her visit.

The short, round old lady attempted to fix her scraggly salt-and-pepper hair while looking at Johndor, smiling. "Thumbeline has given me permission," she said. Adjusting a black scarf around her neck to cover her messy hair, she turned away from Johndor to look at the queen who stood quietly listening next to Johndor.

"I'm quite certain it was not permission, but a challenge she gave you," Johndor said assertively.

Carmile grabbed hold of Lilac's hands. Johndor reached to break the grip.

"It's okay, Johndor," Lilac said, looking into his eyes. She returned her attention to Carmile, saying "Please come into the study," and ushered her toward a door on the far side of the castle's entry.

Carmile looked back, stretching her fat neck and wiggling her head with a flash of her one tooth at Johndor. Johndor's face flushed red with anger.

Meanwhile, Minna opened the door to Isabella's quarters just a crack and peeked inside. Isabella looked past Bethlynn to see who was at the door. Minna shut the door, waited a few seconds, and opened it slightly again to peek inside. Isabella giggled, then hid under her covers, knowing Minna would repeat it a few more times to make her laugh.

"Is it a fox?" Isabella shouted from underneath the covers, guessing what her surprise might be. Bethlynn and Lauren chuckled.

Minna walked in, waving the flower around like a wand, sending the scent of the gardenia into the air, then placed it back in the vase and held it forward for the ladies to inspect. Bethlynn and Lauren tipped up their noses and took a deep breath.

"So lovely," Bethlynn said excitedly. "I wonder if we can plant a tree. I will be happy to care for it."

"You are silly," Lauren replied. "Lilac would pick all the flowers for herself."

Bethlynn's big smile turned into a grin. "You are right. What was I thinking?"

"Now, now, girls," exclaimed Minna, a hand on Isabella's head so she couldn't jump up and grab the vase from her hand. "Settle down, little one." She placed the bud underneath Isabella's nose.

Isabella giggled at the soft petals tickling her nose. "It's a magic flower," she said. "I will make a wish and it will come true." She closed her eyes and whispered loudly, "I will marry Prince Charming and he will kiss me."

Minna smiled. "Yes, you will, darling. You will have everything you want."

Lauren whispered to Bethlynn, "Takes after her father—a hopeless romantic."

Isabella continued more loudly, "And on my next birthday, I will grow so large, my head will touch the ceiling!"

"Oh dear!" Bethlynn said, quickly straightening her shoulders in shock at the funny outburst.

"Yes, you will, darling. Yes, you will," Minna said as she softly tapped the child on the head with the flower as if placing a magic spell.

Minna returned the flower to the vase and placed it on the nightstand next to Isabella's wooden horse. She took Isabella's little hand in hers and walked her downstairs with Bethlynn and Lauren gossiping behind. As they passed, Isabella saw Lilac in the study talking with Carmile.

"Momma, Momma! I got a magic flower, Momma."

"Minna! Please entertain her," the queen snapped.

Bethlynn and Lauren stopped in their tracks behind Minna, in shock that Lilac had spoken to her so roughly. Minna walked faster, dragging a resistant Isabella down the hall, with Lauren gently pushing her forward.

"Bethlynn... Bethlynn!" Lilac shouted. Bethlynn did her best to ignore the queen and kept walking. "Bring us tea, Bethlynn," the queen said. To Carmile, she said, "She makes the best tea."

"A glass of water too, please," Carmile yelled out in a screeching voice.

Isabella, disappointed at her mother's lack of response, reached up for Minna to carry her. Minna tried, but feeling weak and exhausted, gestured for Bethlynn to pick Isabella up.

Isabella whimpered, "Is that witch going to hurt my momma? I'm scared. I want her to leave."

Minna hushed Isabella as she walked faster down the hall and into the kitchen.

"I want her to leave too," Bethlynn whispered in Isabella's ear as she bent down to pick her up. "Perhaps we will put pepper in her tea, and she will sneeze so hard, she will fly out the door."

Isabella laughed. "Do it, Bethlynn. Do it," she cheered.

Lauren nodded, laughing. "Oh my! Now that's not nice," she said as she prepared the teacups on the silver tray.

In the study, Carmile shut the door firmly behind her and walked to Lilac, who sat waiting nervously. Ready to begin, Carmile placed her hand over the crown of Lilac's head, melding her fingers in Lilac's thin, soft, blonde hair. She leaned to one side and whispered in Lilac's ear.

Lilac couldn't make out what Carmile whispered, but she stayed quiet so as not to interrupt. She wondered if the old witch was speaking in another language or just too fast. Carmile pressed harder and harder on the queen's head, pushing it forward.

The door burst open and Bethlynn rushed in, announcing, "Tea time!" in an attempt to break any trance Carmile might have put Lilac in. Carmile looked at Bethlynn with serious eyes and took her seat again.

Bethlynn placed the tray on the tea table between the light blue chairs where the women were sitting. She walked behind Carmile to make her way out of the study and pretended to bop Carmile on the head with a closed fist.

Carmile quickly turned around, having seen Bethlynn's reflection in the mirror on the wall across from her.

Bethlynn quickly brought her arm down and flashed a gentle but fake smile, cocking her head to the side like a sweet debutante. Then she spun on her heels, walked out the door, and closed it a little harder than usual behind her.

Carmile took a small sip of tea. "Mmm... delightful. Bethlynn was such a sweet child... wonder what happened."

She reached for a purple silk pouch hanging from her neck on a black cord and opened it, put something in it, and then secured it closed with a knot. She reached to the silver tray for a sugar cube and dropped it in her tea. She sipped her tea while staring at Lilac with a piercing look.

Lilac's buggy, light brown eyes widened.

"Drink some water," Carmile insisted. "You seem nervous."

Lilac brought the glass of water to her quivering lips and took a small gulp. Carmile set down her tea and quickly untied the knot of the pouch. She pulled out a small brown egg, jumped up, and placed it on Lilac's head. She looked up, closed her eyes, and took a deep breath, then chanted, "Show us today, yesterday, and tomorrow; show yourself, curse; will there be sorrow?" She cracked the egg open into the glass of water Lilac had drank from.

A black glob fell in.

Lilac grimaced. "What is that?"

Carmile brought her face close to the glass and stared in a trance-like state. After several minutes, she turned to Lilac. "Ahh, there is a curse to be removed. I will need to take this glass of water with me. It must be poured at the foot of a bloodroot tree at midnight."

"Yes, yes, take it, please," Lilac said frantically, shifting from side to side in her chair.

Carmile grabbed the glass. "The bloodroot tree stands on the private land of the Wymiers. They demand payment for use of their tree. Would you like me to finish this?"

"Yes, yes. Will it remove the curse?" Lilac said.

Carmile held the glass high as Lilac looked away, disgusted and frightened by the black glob floating there.

"What begins... must end," she said in a screechy, high-pitched voice. She brought the glass down to her waist and held out her other hand. "Fifty shilling coins to start," she said quickly, back to her normal voice.

"Right away!" Lilac stood up at once and went to open the door. "Johndor! Johndor, come in here at once!"

Carmile slipped her small body under Lilac's arms and out the study doors when she heard Lilac shout for Johndor. "I shall wait outside. A pleasure, Your Majesty."

Johndor passed Carmile on his way to the study and gave her a fierce, evil look. Carmile tried to give a mock curtsy to Johndor, but she lost her balance and performed a rather unattractive gesture while trying to stop the glass from spilling over.

"Damn evil eyes, Johndor," she whispered.

An anxious Lilac ran to Johndor as if he wasn't walking fast enough to meet her. "Quickly, I need fifty shillings to pay Carmile."

"Your Majesty, I beg you. This old owl will rob you blind. Her intentions are—"

Lilac held the sides of her head. "Please, Johndor! Isabella's life is in peril, and we need Maurice back. I will do anything."

"As you wish," Johndor said, then walked away, clicking his tongue.

Lilac paced the hallway impatiently, waiting for Johndor to return with the coins. Ten minutes felt like an hour to Lilac, afraid Carmile would grow tired of waiting and leave.

Johndor returned with the coins wrapped tightly in a piece of cotton cloth and tied with a thin strand of old rope. Johndor was in the habit of saving remnants in a round tin can for which he always found uses eventually. He handed Lilac the small pouch. She quickly realized how tight the knot was and tried to loosen it for Carmile's sake. She looked at Johndor for help.

"Fifty shillings it is," he said, then turned and walked away, ignoring Lilac's subtle request to loosen the knot.

Lilac camouflaged the small sack in the folds of her dress and rushed out to pay the old witch. She did not want Bethlynn or Lauren to see her paying Carmile in order to avoid giving the busybodies more to gossip about. Outside, she found Carmile asking Samuel for a ride back to her cottage in the queen's coach and overheard her saying that she was "on an important mission."

Seeing Lilac, Carmile shouted, "We don't want to drop anything, now do we?" while placing her hand over the top of the glass. Lilac walked over and handed Carmile the small bundle. With a swipe, the old witch grabbed the sack of coins and shoved it down her dress into her brassiere.

Lilac put her hand on Samuel's shoulder. "Please, Samuel, if you would be so kind as to return Carmile to her cottage." Samuel, in disbelief, hesitated at first, then replied by opening the coach door for the old woman.

Carmile stepped in with Samuel's help, as her legs were too short and fat to climb inside on her own. After settling into the seat, she waved a hand for Lilac to come closer to the coach, and when she did, the old witch lowered her head and whispered in a low tone, "You must see me in seven days' time. I will be waiting."

She sat up and turned her head away from Lilac, shouting at Samuel,

"Quickly, before nightfall."

The coach set off through the path in the forest. As soon as the castle was out of view, Carmile held up the glass with the disturbing black glob. She pulled the mint-colored curtain away from the coach window, stuck her hand out, and let the glass drop to the ground.

"Royalty... bunch of fools."

Chapter 12

Thegolden glare of the sun rose up through the peculiar Nokbershire forest trees. Delicate silver beams of light peeped through the thatched cottage windows, magnifying bits of dust floating in mid-air.

The rays awakened Maurice. He sat up quickly when he realized where he was. Maggy Mae was standing in the doorway, watching him. She was afraid he would try to leave again and needed him now more than ever. Having taken her innocence, leaving her alone without Nan Marguarite was not an option.

"I've made some tea," she said, her voice breaking at the intimidating look of confusion the king gave her. She walked out of the room to fetch the tea from the kitchen. She freely added more of the potion.

Maurice looked around for his boots. When he didn't see them, he called out, "My boots?"

His scratchy voice startled Maggy Mae, who was stirring the tea in the kitchen. She had placed the king's boots outside the back door to dry. "I will fetch them right away." She returned to the room and handed him the tea with shaking hands.

He scratched his head and sniffed the tea, which reminded him all too well of the smell that had repelled Isiah in the forest. He took just one taste, then put it down quickly and ran out the door, having remembered the cruel reality of what happened to his steed. There lay Isiah, dead, with flies hovering around his stiff body.

Maurice let out a big sigh and gulped, trying to hold back his tears. Maggy Mae ran into the living room with Maurice's boots in hand, noticing the front door was open. She glanced at the almost full teacup and snatched it up from the table.

"Your boots and your tea," she said, handing both to him. She looked down at Isiah and quickly turned away, disturbed by the sight of the dead horse.

"How am I to bury him?" Maurice asked. "I cannot move him alone. How will I get back home?" He let out a sigh of emotional pain and surrender.

"Here," she said, handing him the tea. "I've got an idea."

Maurice sat on the floor next to Isiah and sipped the tea.

Maggy Mae sat down next to him. "The farmer's sons are due to come to deliver the aliment. I'm sure for a few shillings, they will be more than happy to help."

Maurice handed her back the tea and started putting his boots on.

Maggy Mae tried not to be obvious while taking a quick glimpse into the half-empty teacup. "Shall I pour you some more?" she said.

Maurice stepped into the second boot and stretched them both up his calves, then walked back into the house. He opened the wooden trunk, painted sparingly in a rose color, reached in, and grabbed all the scraps of rags and coverlets at once. He walked back out and wrapped Isiah's body. The thought of having to bury Isiah in such a disenchanted foreign land made his body quiver.

He walked to the edge of the forest, circling the periphery, looking for any marked path out. He returned to the curious site where the thick black muck had settled. It was the only obvious path out of the woods.

He walked through, careful not to venture too deep into the forest and lose his way. He spent all day trying to find a way out. Come twilight, having had no success, Maurice returned to the cottage.

Maggy Mae, knowing he wouldn't get too far without a horse, had taken it upon herself to cook a ham. It was the last of the meat. Nan Marguarite would not have served it until the farmer boys arrived with more.

With a ravaging hunger, Maurice unapologetically ate most of the food, not noticing that Maggy Mae barely touched hers. Instead, she just played with her food in angst, rhythmically tapping the silver fork on the brass platter.

Maggy Mae prepared Maurice a bath after dinner. He accepted, being very careful to avoid any possible romantic encounter. Maggy Mae had other intentions. She planned a seduction Maurice would not be able to resist.

Yet he did resist. All he could think about was Isiah. She pressed her body close against his as she patted him dry and reached her lips to his. "Please, fair maiden, let's not get entrapped by each other's grief."

Maurice quickly dressed and sat on the big armchair, crossing his feet over the footstool. There he fell asleep for the rest of the night. He awoke the next morning slumped over the arm of the chair with a stiff neck, hearing voices off in the distance. He rubbed his neck with one hand and his eyes with the other. The voices got closer. Quickly, he got his boots on and stumbled from the chair to the window. He saw three farmer boys standing around Isiah. Maurice rushed out the front door.

The farmer boys recognized Maurice, but said nothing.

"Good morning, lads. Assist me, I beg. My horse has died, and I need help to bury him. I also need a ride back to Fleurham. I will reward a hefty amount."

The boys smiled at this confirmation that it was King Maurice after all—a scruffy, disturbed version, but King Maurice nonetheless—and continued to offer him silence in loyalty.

The eldest brother introduced himself with a firm handshake. "The name's Thomas, and these are my brothers Roger and Finley. We can most definitely use a reward, sir," he said as they walked back to the cart to untie the rope holding the canopy down. Roger moved quickly to grab the other end of the rope as Finley began to unload the fare.

Maggy Mae stood nervously at the doorway, watching. She thought, *I can't let him leave. What will I do if he tries to leave with the boys?*

Thomas found a spot on the south side of the cottage with plenty of earth. "Right here's a good spot," he called to his brothers and Maurice in a Cornish accent.

He spotted a shovel leaning against the frame of the back door, grabbed it, and began digging a hole. The soil was still somewhat soft from the heavy downpours of recent days, making it easier to dig through.

Roger and Finley strategically placed the rope around the horse's body. Maurice bent over to help, but Roger, confident Maurice was King of Fleurham, refused his help. "We got this, sire..." He nervously cleared his throat. "Sir," he corrected.

Maurice took no notice of the comment as Roger's country accent was quite thick and he'd spoken rather quickly.

Roger rolled up the sleeves of his tunic, and Finley straightened his flat hat. They began dragging Isiah off the front porch. Thomas saw his brothers having difficulty moving the heavy steed and walked over to help them. He unwrapped the top layer of rags, tied on another piece of rope he grabbed from the cart, and pulled with the boys.

Maurice followed them. At the side of the hole, he knelt before Isiah and whispered, "Sorry, ole boy" with no tears this time, just a stoic farewell.

"Alright now, sir?" Thomas said to Maurice.

Maurice nodded in agreement and the boys gently allowed Isiah's body to fill the earthy void. They removed the ropes tied around his body. Finley removed his flat hat and put it over his heart, then mouthed a few words that couldn't be heard, placed his flat hat back on his head, and began to slide mounds of earth over Isiah. Thomas used the shovel, working quickly to bring an end to this heartbreaking event for Maurice.

Finley ran into the forest and returned with a small purple flower. He handed it to Maurice, who made the sign of the cross with the flower and threw it in as Thomas and Roger continued to shovel dirt in the hole.

Maurice glanced at the cottage, feeling resentment toward the missing Marguarite, knowing those white cubes were to blame for Isiah's death. Maggy Mae stood watching from the back door, nervously rubbing a piece of her lacy garment and contemplating a plan to keep Maurice with her. She signaled with her hand for him to come to her.

Maurice stared at her, trying to figure out what she needed him for. With time to kill while the boys finished the job, he said, "I'll be just a minute, boys. Then we can be on our way," and walked over to the back door.

Maggy Mae stared at him nervously. "I need you to help me fetch something from the hidden vault under the house."

Maurice looked at her suspiciously.

She stuttered as she continued, "It... it... It's to pay the boys for the fare. Nan kept all the shillings hidden in there." She turned and led Maurice around the cottage, moved some stones from over a hidden door, then slid her shoe around the edge to uncover the handle. Maurice bent over and pulled it open, discovering a ladder reaching at least ten feet down.

"At the bottom, there is a shelf with a wooden box," she said.

Maurice made his way down carefully. "It's pitch black in here," his words echoed.

"I will fetch the lantern," Maggy Mae yelled down, then carefully closed the vault door and walked quickly to the boys, who were making space in the cart for Maurice. She gave them a handful of gold coins. "This is for the fare and for helping with the steed."

The boys looked at each other—except for Thomas. He looked Maggy Mae in her eyes.

"We will be traveling for some time and won't need your services for a bit," she said, turning away.

"The gentleman," Thomas said. "He asked us to take him back to Fleurham."

Maggy Mae gave Thomas a stern look. "He has changed his mind. You may be on your way. Thank you. Nice day," she said as she scuttled away quickly.

Thomas shrugged his shoulders as he turned to his brothers. "We'd probably never find our way there anyway."

Maggy Mae ran through the house, quickly lit a lantern, and returned to the vault. She lifted the door and hung the lantern from a nail on the edge of the opening.

"There is no chest in here... not even a shelf. Only a couple of old dusty diaries," Maurice said, raising his voice to make sure Maggy Mae could hear him. "I will pay the boys for your fare." He started to climb out.

In a panic, Maggy Mae let the door close to trap Maurice again. She ran to make sure the farmer boys had left the property. They were at the edge of the forest, moving slowly away. As she turned back toward the house, she noticed the vault door lifting up slowly. Checking again, she could see the boys still in the distance. She ran and stepped on the door, pushing it down with the weight of her body to stop Maurice from coming out. She checked again to make sure the boys were out of view, then pulled the vault door open.

"Well," Maurice said. "I can't thank you enough for the hospitality."

Maggy Mae stood nodding at him with a blank expression on her face. Her heart raced in anticipation of his reaction at finding that the farmer boys had left him behind.

Maurice walked around the cottage with an eager, yet modest smile of relief to be leaving the ill-fated estate. He looked left and right, not seeing the boys anywhere. His heart beat faster. He ran to the edge of the woods. He shouted for the boys. Enraged, he kicked the dirt, trapping his foot underneath a tree root buried in the black muck, causing him to be thrown to the ground. Falling on his left shoulder, he let out a loud cry of pain and anger. He called for the boys louder. The sound of nothing but silence in return infuriated him further.

He turned to Maggy Mae, who was staring at him in confusion from midway between the cottage and the woods. She hesitated, thinking he might know she was to blame. Pretending to be surprised, she ran to his rescue.

This was her evil-doing, he thought, and considered tripping her as she got closer. Perhaps she will hit her head hard enough to put her to her death.

She reached him and knelt into the thick mud to pull his boot out from under the root that had him trapped. "Are you alright?" She pulled hard on the tough, rubbery branches, trying to free him. "Where are the boys?" she asked innocently.

"Where are the boys, you ask?" Maurice said angrily. "You tell me... where are the boys?"

She looked at Maurice straight in the eyes. "They have left you?" She released his foot from the root and helped him up, then called out, "Thomas! Thomas! I will go look for them." She started toward the dense forest.

Maurice grabbed her arm. "Don't. You will get lost."

She turned around and caressed his shoulder where he was holding it in obvious pain.

He looked her in the eyes and suddenly felt deep gratitude for her actions. The thought of her evil-doing quickly vanished. They walked back to the cottage.

Maggy Mae prepared warm rags and placed them over Maurice's undressed shoulder. While he rested, she steeped tea, smiling with a deep feeling of joy and victory.

Finley stopped the horses. "Wasn't it a bit strange? He seemed desperate to leave."

Thomas moved over and took the reigns from Finley, urging the horses to continue, shaking his head in disbelief. "You read too much into things that don't concern you, Fin."

Chapter 13

The castle remained in a state of distress over the missing king. The tension was thick among everyone, and the staff acted in obedience and compassion for the queen and Isabella out of pity. Johndor, however, continued displaying his disappointment at the queen's decision to allow Carmile into the private matters of the castle, constantly clicking his tongue whenever he saw her.

He walked into the kitchen with a white silk rag, filthy with old dirt stains, which would not come out, regardless of Minna's scrubbing.

When Isabella saw him, she jumped out of her seat, throwing the last bit of cranberry scone she'd been eating on the table. Dropping crumbs all the way, she ran to Johndor excitedly. "Are we going to pick cherries?"

Minna, busy washing the dishes, looked back with a big smile.

Bethlynn said, "Remember the queen's orders."

Johndor spoke with an assertive, yet nonchalant tone. "What is this order you speak of?" He pulled down on Isabella's lower eyelids to check the color of the blood vessels in her eyes. "Hmm, a bit paler than usual," he said softly to himself. Isabella held her breath and stayed still even though Johndor's rough fingertips scratched her soft face. He released her eyelids, and she immediately began jumping with joy.

"What order?" Minna asked.

Bethlynn replied sarcastically, "Isabella is now a prisoner in this castle. She is not to see the light of day again."

Isabella cupped Johndor's hands with hers. "I go wherever Johndor goes," she said.

Johndor held Isabella's hand and trailed her out of the kitchen with him. "Lilac can take that up with me," he said.

Bethlynn widened her eyes as she scrubbed a tablecloth in a tub of warm water. "I don't want to be around for that."

"Bring me back some cherries," Lauren shouted in a singing voice from the kitchen pantry, where she was organizing burlap bags of potatoes.

Minna looked at Johndor, hoping he might change his mind. She dared say nothing. She had great respect for her husband.

Isabella skipped through the hallway out the doors, singing, "We're going to "pick" cherries, we're going to pick—"

"Shhh," Johndor whispered, holding his pointer finger to his lips and looking around to make sure Lilac didn't hear her. "We must not let the cherries hear us."

Isabella gasped as she slapped her little hand over her mouth, then started skipping again.

At the sound of the front door shutting, Minna sighed.

Bethlynn shrugged her shoulders. "A brave one, he is."

Isabella skipped into the woods with Johndor. A journey through the woods had always been Isabella's daily highlight. She looked forward to it, as did Johndor. He would teach her the different leaves of bushes and trees and instruct her on the benefits of each. The next day, he would test her. Isabella loved the challenge. Johndor had a special place in his heart for the child, and feeling she was safest in his care, he would not deprive her of their daily outing.

Back in the castle kitchen, the women talked nervously, hoping Lilac would not notice Isabella had gone off with Johndor.

"She's as cheeky as her mother," Bethlynn said as she hung up the damp tablecloth.

"Let's sew her a new gown. She has outgrown that one, don't you think, Minna?"

Lauren stuck her head in the kitchen and said, "She won't part with it. She thinks she's a faery when she wears it. Surely she will come back with a flower halo on her head and a branch as a wand, turning everyone into animals as she makes her way back to the castle."

Bethlynn said, "Certainly you will be turned into a talking parrot, Lauren."

Lauren threw an empty burlap bag at Bethlynn. It landed on her sister's head and covered her face. The three women broke out in laughter.

Suddenly they heard the front doors shut loudly. The three women froze, fearing Lilac had found Johndor out. The tension in their bodies melted as they saw Johndor and Isabella walk in the kitchen—and then returned again when they saw Isabella's swollen eyes.

"Seems highly unlikely, but looks like she's had some kind of allergic reaction," Johndor said, puzzled at this unusual incident. "I will be back with some chrysanthemum. Start boiling the water," he said to Minna as he walked out of the kitchen.

Isabella giggled, looking up at Minna and pointing at her right eye. "I can't open my eye."

The three ladies looked at each other, afraid of Lilac's reaction. "We shall not say she's gone out," Minna said to Bethlynn and Lauren. Minna reached high in the cupboard and hid something small in her hand. She kneeled down in front of Isabella and gently dropped a caramel candy in her mouth. "Deary, you must not tell your mum you've been out with Johndor. Can you keep this special secret?"

"Yes Minna, Lilac will never know our secret," she said, exaggerating her chewing as she tried to break down the candy.

Chapter 14

Two long months passed and Maurice was growing dispirited, missing his royal life and worrying about his family in Fleurham. He often wondered why no one had come looking for him.

He stood a few feet away from the edge of the forest, searching for a way out. Although he had grown to appreciate Maggy Mae and had used his unexpected stay to have his way with the young lady, his intention had remained to return to the castle. He scratched his head, trying to understand why the farmer boys had not returned in two months. Food would begin to run low if they did not return soon.

He stood between the two trees he was certain Isiah had entered through. He grabbed a few stones and branches to mark his way. Past attempts had been unsuccessful, as the rain and winds moved and covered the branches and stones he'd used as markers each time, leaving him lost for hours. But today he was determined to find his way out. He had taken a knife with him to carve an X into the trees on his right every twenty-five steps. He took his first twenty-five steps, walked to the closest tree to his right, and drove the knife into the tree trunk. The knife bounced back. He tried again and again. With every stab, the knife bounced back and hardly made a mark. He took a few steps back, clenched his jaw, and ran towards the tree, knife in hand, ready to pierce it with all his might. As the tip of the knife touched the tree trunk, the trunk became soft and the entire blade of the knife was swallowed, leaving only the handle sticking out. He pulled the handle with all his might, but it did not budge. He wiggled it from side to side, grabbed it with both hands, placed his right foot on the tree for leverage, and pulled back with all his might. The handle broke off, sending Maurice to the ground on his backside, the knife handle still clenched in both hands.

Maurice stood up, enraged, and threw the handle at the tree, sending a flock of birds flying. He stared at the birds in amazement. *How peculiar*, he thought. *Peach-colored birds, ay? Well, what do you know?* The birds fluttered their shiny satin wings, floating just above the tree. He walked over to take a better look. The flock of small birds moved about a yard ahead, matching Maurice's pace. Maurice stopped. The flock stopped. He took a few steps. The flock moved ahead a few feet.

"I don't mean to scare you off," he called up to the birds, cupping his mouth to direct his voice at the flock.

The birds moved up a few more feet.

Maurice stood watching. The flock flew toward him, chirping a high-pitched sound, then flew a few feet ahead and waited.

Fearful of getting lost, Maurice turned around and headed back. The flock flew into a tree, disappearing within the leaves.

Maurice reached the cottage and sat on the floor by the door, not wanting to enter. He sat thinking about the peculiar birds and the trunk of the tree swallowing the knife. He stared at the trees, thinking about Isiah's lifeless body, about Isabella and the arrow, about the castle without his presence, and about what his life had become over the past two months.

"I will find a way out. I will find a way out," he whispered, leaning his head against the door. He began to pray for guidance.

Maurice nodded off and dreamed of the peculiar birds lifting him by his garments with their tiny beaks. As he began to lift up in the air, he dropped from the birds' clasp with a loud thump, waking him up. He quickly realized the thump was not in the dream and rushed inside the cottage.

Maggy Mae lay on the floor, trying to get up.

Maurice lifted her up and walked her to the purple, rounded armchair close to the fireplace. "What happened? Are you alright?" he asked as he sat her down gently and propped her feet up on a wooden footstool.

"Had a dizzy spell, that's all," she answered meekly, arms across her belly as if she felt sick. She got up quickly and ran outside, retching until her stomach was empty of all the food she had eaten earlier that day. Maurice stared from the doorway, then ran to the kitchen and back out with a wet rag to wipe her face. He carried her to bed and tended to her all night, continuously changing out the metal bucket he had placed next to her bed.

Both, fully exhausted, finally fall asleep just before dawn.

With only a couple of hours of sleep, an exhausted Maurice snored loudly as he lay fully dressed on the bed, which was too small for a man of his size. He heard a far-off galloping and squinted his eyes. Isiah was racing toward him! He ran to the steed and thrust his boot into the foot strap, straddling Isiah in one quick jump. Isiah dashed toward the forest edge, and Maurice slid off and hit the ground. The white horse ran off into the woods.

"Isiah!" Maurice yelled, just as he felt a soft hand touch his face. He jerked his eyes open, finding Maggy Mae kneeling on the floor next to him and gently caressing his face.

"You're dreaming. You fell off the bed. Are you alright?" she said.

He took a deep breath and closed his eyes. He lay still until his racing heart returned to normal rhythm. He tugged at his ears, still hearing the galloping. The sun was rising, and its light began to peek into the bedroom, so he pulled himself up and stumbled to the basin. He splashed water on his face and rubbed his ears again. The galloping became louder, then came to a halt.

Three strong knocks at the door startled Maurice back to his senses. He looked up at Maggy Mae, who had managed to drag her weak body back into the bed. Pale-faced and barely able to hold her eyes open, she faced the sunlight peeking into the small room from the other side. Feeble and exhausted, she struggled to lift her head up to look out the window. The sunlight's glare beamed on her gaunt face for a second before her head collapsed back on the soft pillow.

Maurice quickly walked to the door in hopes that it might be the farmer boys. Opening the door, he found an older man of medium build with thick brown hair and bushy eyebrows scrunched into a mean look on his face. The man took a step inside, forcing Maurice to make way for his bold entrance.

"Who may you be?" the man demanded.

"The name is Maurice, and you are?"

"Where's Maggy Mae... my daughter?"

A retching sound from the back room signaled that Maggy Mae was sick again. The man quickly made his way to the bedroom. Maurice began to follow, but then stopped and looked out the window. A large black horse stood loosely tied outside. He was tempted to jump on the horse and flee.

Surely this horse will know his way out, he thought.

Maggy Mae's crying broke Maurice out of his lucid thinking and brought him back to the surreal present moment, just as Maggy Mae's

74

voice, her touch, or her scent always did.

He looked into the room. The man was sitting on the bed, holding Maggy Mae, and they were speaking very low. Maurice tried to make out what they were saying, soon realizing they were speaking a different dialect. Maggy Mae kept nodding her head and repeating "roi," meaning king in French. The man laid Maggy Mae down gently and moved her hair away from her face, then stood up slowly and walked to the front door.

"I will go for help. Do not leave her alone!" he told Maurice assertively.

Maurice nodded in agreement as he saw the man out the door, then stood on the porch to watch which path the horse took. Maurice ran toward the forest edge just as the horse entered the woods, but was taken aback by Maggy Mae's call and ran back to the cottage.

In a feeble voice Maggy Mae whispered, "Water please." She wrapped one arm around her waist and the other around her breasts, hung her head down, and began to sob.

"Father went to find Nan Marguarite. She can cure me." She grabbed the hem of her dress and dried her eyes and face.

Maurice brushed her hair out of her face with his fingers, then kissed her head and held her hands. He brought his voice down to a very gentle tone and said, "When my daughter becomes ill, Johndor, my trusted steward, makes her a tea from a plant. I have learned to recognize it. I shall go out and look for it in the woods."

Maggy Mae's face suddenly became very serious. "You have a daughter?" Her voice sounded ready to break into tears.

"Yes!" Maurice replied proudly.

"And a wife, I imagine?" she said in a disappointed tone.

"Yes, yes, which is why I must get back," Maurice said.

Maggy Mae turned on her side, holding her dress to her face to hide her tears of jealousy and anger. Her body jerked from her effort to hold in her emotions. Maurice gently turned her face toward him. She resisted in defiance, and he took his hand away, realizing that she had mistaken his inevitable stay for one of a romantic nature.

He sat speechless on the bed. *I should have taken the horse,* he thought.

Maggy Mae continued to cry. He offered her water. She refused. She clung to the bunched up folds of her lavender-colored dress, crying into the soft fabric.

"I will go find the plant now." Maurice stood and slowly walked out to the woods.

Chapter 15

Two hours after Maurice set out in search of the plant, he still dared not venture too deeply into the forest. He had passed the plant several times, but had taken no notice of it. His concentration had been focused on how to escape. He had decided he would explain to Maggy Mae's father how he had ended up stranded, certain the man would understand and help him. He walked to Isiah's burial site, bent down on one knee, brushed the dirt off the stones, and shed a few tears. Closing his eyes, he tried to erase the memory of a lifeless Isiah. He soon heard galloping coming closer, and the voice of men speaking loudly broke the king's trance.

Maggy Mae's father had returned with an older gentleman sitting behind him on the horse.

Maggy Mae's father jumped off his horse first, then helped the older, white-haired gentleman off. The short, round-bodied man was dressed all in black. He wobbled toward the house behind Maggy Mae's father.

Maurice walked slowly away from Isiah's burial site to keep his distance from Maggy Mae's father. Taking his time, he walked toward the cottage behind the men.

The short man turned around and waited for Maurice to get closer.

He looked into Maurice's eyes. He paused, then bowed his head in royal greeting. "Benjamin Tottle, physician, at your service."

Maurice stared back, thinking he seemed entirely familiar.

The three men walked into the house. Maggy Mae's father left Maurice and the doctor in the front room while he went to speak with his daughter, but he soon reappeared in the doorway of her room, calling for Dr. Tottle.

"Right away, Mr. Morchedeaux," Dr. Tottle replied, then wobbled his way to the room. Maurice stood by the door, watching Maggy Mae's gaunt pale face, and feeling uninvited.

When he entered her room, Maggy Mae smiled at Dr. Tottle, who had been attending to her since she was born. He had delivered her to the Morchedeaux family twenty-eight years earlier during an unforgettably sad event. Maggy Mae's mother had died during the delivery, and the newborn would not have lived either, had Dr. Tottle arrived even five minutes later than he did. He smiled, patted Maggy Mae's sweaty head, and asked ever so kindly for privacy. Mr. Morchedeaux nodded in agreement and stepped outside, closing the door behind him while giving Maurice a dirty look of disapproval.

Restless, the two men sat on the set of armchairs in the sitting room without looking at each other or saying a word, anxious about Maggy Mae's condition. Maurice recited in his mind how he would ask Mr. Morchedeaux for help returning to Fleurham.

Mr. Morchedeaux broke the silence, unable to contain his suspicions any longer. "Why have you come to Nokbershire?"

"By accident... Mr. Morchedeaux, is it?" Maurice replied, indignant at being treated as a common man. "My horse became afraid under a great storm in the woods and somehow ended up here. Marguarite was kind enough to offer hospitality and let us stay until the storm passed."

Mr. Morchedeaux glared at Maurice as he listened.

"The next morning as I was ready to leave, I found my steed had died. The farm boys offered to take me back to Fleurham but—"

"Fleurham?" Mr. Morchedeaux said. He knew about the conditions of Fleurham. The kingdom was in process of being rebuilt after the old royal town of Cuvington had been burned down.

Distressed, Maurice gazed at Mr. Morchedeaux's eyes. There was something about his look that made Maurice uncomfortable. He took a deep breath of courage and dared to ask. "Mr. Morchedeaux, I can compensate you generously if you would get me back to Fleurham. My family needs me, and I can only imagine they must be worried sick at my disappearance."

The bedroom door shut and Dr. Tottle walked toward the two men. Mr. Morchedeaux stood up.

"Please sit, Charles," Dr. Tottle insisted.

Mr. Morchedeaux sat slowly, staring at Dr. Tottle with a grim look on his face. Dr. Tottle turned to Maurice, nodded at him, and then looked at Mr. Morchedeaux.

"Maggy Mae is with child."

Mr. Morchedeaux jumped straight up and angrily said, "She is with child?!" He kicked a chair out of the way to make his way toward Maggy Mae. Dr. Tottle grabbed Mr. Morchedeaux's arm. "You will do her and the child harm. Please sit and pull yourself together."

Frozen by this news, Maurice had not imagined his situation could become more complicated than it already was.

Mr. Morchedeaux stared at Maurice, flaring his nostrils in anger. "What did you do with Nan Marguarite?"

Maurice replied, "I did nothing with Nan Marguarite. She never returned."

Dr. Tottle interrupted, looking at Maurice with a feeling of sorrow. "You seem healthy, and Maggy Mae is also of good health. There should be nothing to worry about. I will visit every full moon to check on her health. I now have to tend to a very sick child in Gregoria. Mr. Morchedeaux, if you would be so kind." He turned to Maurice and bowed. As he brought his head back up, he gave Maurice a look of sympathy, knowing the road ahead would be one of tribulation and anguish, given the history of Maggy Mae's ancestors. Dr. Tottle stepped outside.

Mr. Morchedeaux stepped up to Maurice and whispered indignantly, "And you want to leave? Ha! I dare you! It will cost you your life... and I will take it myself with my bare hands. You wouldn't be the first!" He pointed to the room. "Now, go take care of your wife-to-be!" He walked to the front door and pulled it open with all his force, slamming the doorknob against the wall behind it. Muttering angry words, he walked out, signaling to Dr. Tottle that he was coming.

Maurice took a deep breath. His eyes welled up with tears of anger and confusion. He threw a powerful punch to the wall next to the door, making the windows shake. He let out a raging growl. Clenching his jaws and fists, he walked into the room to find Maggy Mae with her head dug into the pillow to hide her sobbing. He was tempted to yell at her, but realized she too was a victim of her father's domination.

He knelt on the floor in front of her. "I cannot stay here. Do you understand? I have a family and a kingdom to rebuild."

Between sobs, she said, "You... did... this... to me."

Maurice sat on the bed and pulled her up to face him, holding her shoulders tightly. "I will make sure you are taken care of. I cannot stay. I cannot stay... here."

Maggy Mae grabbed his hands with her shaking hands. "I beg you, please. Don't leave me... I am too ill. I cannot take care of myself. Nan is gone. Please... please."

Frustrated, Maurice nodded in agreement as he gently squeezed her hands. "I will stay. I will stay with you until you have recovered. But have no doubt, after that I will leave." He stood up quickly.

"Where are you going?" she asked fearfully.

"To find the plant. It will make you better right away."

Chapter 16

Two difficult months passed without knowing about the king. Isabella had continuously fallen unusually ill. She suffered severe body aches during cold evenings, leaving her with painful, stiff, immovable joints. Bouts of digestive disorders and nightmares had caused many sleepless nights for Minna and Johndor. The recent concern over Isabella's health had affected all involved, as they had to take turns nursing her overnight.

A frustrated Queen Lilac aimlessly roamed the castle halls, blaming Isabella's ailments on the curse. And now that Isabella was of school age and was displaying learning difficulties, Lilac's frustration grew even more.

The sun had risen hours ago, awakening Lilac from a restless night much later than usual. She quietly sneaked into Isabella's room so as to not wake her and attempted to change her from her sleeping garments to a new white gown she knew Isabella would not approve of. Lilac had designed it and had Bethlynn sew it for her for a special occasion.

Isabella kicked, half awake, with her eyes still shut. She squinted and yelled at the sight of her mother. "Where's Minna? What is that dress? I don't like it... it's ugly!" she yelled, fighting it off as her mother forced it on her.

With arms stretched up, Isabella let out a muffled yell for Minna from inside her dress. "Minna! Help me!"

"Look at the pearl buttons. They are darling," Lilac said. "We are going on an outing today."

Interested now, Isabella jumped up on the bed and said excitedly, "Where, where? Is Minna coming?"

"Minna is resting today. She's exhausted and not well," Lilac replied.

"No, Minna, Minna, Minna!" Isabella sang, jumping up and down on the bed.

"Settle down, Isabella, you'll start coughing again—and I need to put on your socks."

Isabella plopped down on the bed and reached her foot up to Lilac's nose. Lilac pushed it down quickly and said sternly, "No, Isabella. No games."

Isabella kicked her foot out again toward Lilac's face. "But Minna always smells my stinky feet and then nibbles my toes."

Lilac pulled Isabella's legs and held them down, staring intently at the scar below the right knee. She sighed and whispered to herself, "This is all my fault."

Isabella quietly scrunched up her small button nose with a look of disgust, slowly analyzing the dress her mother had tricked her into.

Johndor opened the door, startling the both out of their trance. Isabella pulled her legs out of Lilac's grip and cheered, "My tea, my tea!"

Johndor carried the special white and red teacup with gold stars to Isabella. Lilac stood up and pushed the teacup away. "Oh, no, no. She will soil her dress."

Johndor pushed right past Lilac's hand and gave Isabella the tea. He stood at the head of her bed, ensuring Lilac would not attempt to take the tea away. Lilac reached over quickly and wrapped the sleeping garment around Isabella's chest like a bib.

"You're choking me," Isabella said, faking a hoarse voice.

Lauren's singing was heard coming down the hallway. "I've got blueberry scones, blueberry scones, blueberry scones... I've got blueberry scones..." And as she appeared in the doorway and fixed her eyes on Isabella, she finished with, "All for you!"

"For me!" Isabella cheered. "All for me!"

Lauren sat on the bed and held a small burgundy plate with the warm blueberry scone perfectly centered for Isabella. Lilac brought her hands to her head in dread. "For God's sake, Lauren, feed it to her so she doesn't ruin her dress!"

Isabella opened her mouth and stuck out her tongue. Johndor leaned in closer to check it for any signs of indigestion, as he did every morning.

Isabella had managed to eat most of the scone without dropping a crumb on her dress. Lauren held the last small piece between her thumb and index finger and put it in the child's mouth. Isabella bit down before Lauren could move her fingers out of the way and dug her big, crooked front teeth, which were finally coming through, into Lauren's fingers.

"Ouch!" Lauren yelled as the piece of scone fell onto the garment wrapped around Isabella.

Lilac, who was discreetly looking out the window, darted to Isabella's side at the sound of Lauren's yelp. "Alright! That's enough now!" she yelled while pushing away the plate and teacup and pulling Isabella out of her bed.

Isabella ran to the basin to wash her face and rinse her mouth, as Johndor always stressed the importance of keeping the mouth clean. Lilac pulled her by the hand, stopping her. "No, Isabella. That's not necessary. You're only a little girl." The queen led the child out the door.

Johndor clicked his tongue against his teeth in disagreement and followed Lilac and Isabella down the hall. He pulled gently on Isabella's long golden hair, trying to get her attention. She turned around, and

Johndor stuck that last piece of scone in her mouth. She flashed a big smile at Johndor, dropping small crumbs of scone down the front of her dress. Johndor blurted out a laugh of victory.

Lauren, who walked next to Johndor, sighed at the sight of the crumbs falling, then dashed back into Isabella's room to avoid hearing Lilac's frenzy.

At the bottom of the stairs, Lilac told Isabella to wait with Johndor and walked into the study. She returned with Isabella's most dreaded object: the heavy silver hairbrush. Isabella held her head with both hands and shrieked as she ran to hide behind Johndor—but even Johndor agreed, the princess needed to brush her tangled, messy hair. He squatted down to her level and promised her one copper pence if she let her hair get brushed. Lilac waited, tapping the brush on her right hip. Isabella scrunched her eyebrows at her mother and poked out her tongue.

"Isabella!" Lilac yelled.

"Can Minna do it?" Isabella asked with pleading eyes. "Or Bethlynn?" she asked excitedly as she saw her walk out of the study.

"I will do it. Give me here." Bethlynn said firmly, holding her hand out to Lilac for the brush. Lilac gently slapped the brush on Bethlynn's open palm, "Fine, you do it, but don't take forever as usual. We've got to move on." Bethlynn rolled her eyes as she gave Lilac her back. Lilac sighed in frustration, shaking her head, then turning and making her way to the front doors. "I shall wait in the coach," she yelled as she made her way down the hall.

Bethlynn brushed Isabella's hair and discreetly swiped away the crumbs from her dress.

Isabella had not been out of the castle more than once or twice in two months because of her ailments and the weather, as Lilac was certain that the rain and cold air would cause her to fall ill and would claim her life.

Johndor took Isabella by the hand and walked her outside, toward the waiting carriage. "Tomorrow we will return to the woods and pick cherries," he said.

Isabella smiled and looked up at Johndor. "Where are we going now?"

"Not sure, little one. You must ask your mother," Johndor replied, knowing full well where Lilac was headed.

He helped her into the coach. Lilac settled Isabella next to her as Johndor closed the door.

"Carmile's, Your Majesty?" Samuel asked before stepping up to the sitting box.

"Yes, Samuel, to Carmile's. You know the way."

Having taken Lilac to Carmile's almost every day for the last month, Samuel rolled his eyes and whispered under his breath, "With my eyes closed."

"Where are we going, Momma?" Isabella asked sweetly.

"We are going to visit Carmile. She is like a nana. She will make you well again."

"But I'm not sick, Momma."

Lilac looked at Isabella and sternly said, "Yes, Isabella. There is always something wrong with you, and you are starting to look like a sickly girl. Ever since you got hit with that cursed arrow. We must rid you of this curse so you can have a good life. We must not talk about it... it is bad to."

"But, Momma, I don't want to go there. I want to stay with Minna and Johndor."

"Oh, you must not forget to collect that pence from Johndor," Lilac said.

Isabella looked back at Johndor becoming smaller in the distance. She tried to open the coach door while calling for Johndor and waving her hand.

Lilac pulled Isabella back and pinned her legs under her own to stop her from moving. "Are you daft?" she yelled. "You could have fallen out!"

Isabella crossed her arms and spat, "No! I am not daft. I'm very smart!"

"Then we must go see Carmile! Faster, Samuel," she said, leaning her head through the front opening of the coach.

Isabella flopped on her mother's lap and began to cry.

Frustrated, Lilac snapped, "Isabella, you are hurting my legs." Then she sat Isabella back straight in her seat.

Isabella soon fell asleep, slumped sideways. Lilac was thankful for the quiet over the two-hour journey to Carmile's abode. Lilac began to move Isabella gently to wake her as Samuel approached Carmile's house. The uninviting, ragged little shack was dark and unkempt, with slabs of wood nailed in wrong directions in an unsuccessful repair attempt.

Lilac waited for Samuel to open the coach door. "If you would be so kind as to help me with Isabella. She must be fatigued again."

Samuel carried Isabella out of the coach as she rubbed her eyes half-awake, and stood her up, holding her teetering body steady with one hand and helping Lilac out with the other.

A half-asleep Isabella stared at the trickling creek just yards away, mesmerized by the melody of the water over the stones. The sun sparkled on the water, resembling shining stars. She waved her hand back and forth, shooing a flying insect.

"What is it Isabella?" Lilac asked nervously.

Isabella yelped, "It's a mosquito!"

Lilac grabbed Isabella and ran to Carmile's front door, knocking politely yet continuously, while guarding Isabella with her dress. There was no answer. Lilac knocked harder. Carmile finally opened the door wide and stood aside for them to enter.

"Eww!" Isabella held her nose. "I'm gonna be sick."

Lilac turned and raised her hand, signaling Samuel permission to leave. He knew the routine. He would return at 3:00 p.m. to bring them back to the castle before nightfall.

As Lilac brought her arm down, she slapped Isabella's little hand off her nose. "Don't be rude, Isabella! Have you no manners?"

Carmile laughed.

Isabella shrunk into her mother's skirt at the sight of Carmile's remaining yellowed tooth and scrunched up the skirt to cover her button nose. Lilac stepped into the house, dragging Isabella with her.

Isabella's breaths became shorter as she grew more fearful of the dimly lit house and Carmile. The windows were boarded over with wood on the outside. The only light was generated by six ivory-colored candles surrounding an urn-like metal container and a glass goblet, holding what looked like dirty water, sitting on a wooden table.

Isabella released her mother's skirt from her face and whined, "I don't feel well. I want to leave."

A frustrated Lilac drew her hand up, cupping her forehead and looking down. Distressed and exhausted, she said, "What is it, Isabella? What do you feel now?" She looked at Carmile. "Do you see what this curse has done to my daughter?"

Isabella whimpered, "I feel scared in my stomach. I don't want to be here." Her voice sounded frail and weak.

Lilac pointed her chin to the ceiling and took a deep breath. "We will leave soon, I promise." She patted Isabella's head gently while trying to loosen the child's small fingers from their tight grip on her skirt. She smiled at Carmile sheepishly, trying to hide her frustration and embarrassment.

Isabella grabbed her mother's arm and jumped up and down, stomping loudly. "Let's go! Let's go!"

"Stop, Isabella! Stop!" Lilac said assertively yet gently so as to not to let on to Carmile how quickly she often lost her temper. Isabella squatted down, grabbed the bottom of her mother's skirt and pulled it up, exposing her mother from the waist down. Lilac grabbed Isabella by the hair, making Isabella lose her balance and fall to the floor.

"Stop, I've said!" Lilac whisper-yelled in Isabella's ear as she stood the child back on her feet. "And stop crying! You are embarrassing me!"

Carmile walked to the bookcase standing next to the door, raised herself up on her tippy toes, reached deep behind a red glass, and pulled out a small rag doll. She handed it to Isabella. "Here you go, Princess. Can you take care of her for a little while?"

Isabella stepped back and looked down at her feet, ignoring Carmile.

Lilac shoved Isabella gently towards Carmile, gesturing that Isabella should take the doll. Apprehensively, Isabella stuck out her thumb and index finger and pinched the doll between her fingers, as if touching something dirty, as she scrunched up her nose and eyebrows.

Carmile ushered Lilac to sit down on a dark blue chair detailed with black tassels hanging from the wooden edges of the seat. Isabella sat on the floor next to the old chair, holding the rag doll with one hand and reaching for the empty spaces where tassels were missing with the other hand. She tucked her head under the chair in search of the missing tassels, then sneezed from the dust collected under the chair.

Lilac shook her head in disappointment. *She must be getting sick again,* she thought. "Isabella, don't sit on the cold floor. Sit on the other chair, please."

"I'm going to be sick, Momma. It smells funny—"

"Why don't you sit outside and get some fresh air?" Carmile said, opening the door.

"But the mosquitos," Lilac said nervously.

Carmile cackled, then said, "Mosquitoes? Those things only happen to bad people. She is a special child. She has abilities, don't you know? We must remove the curse, or her powers will work against her in life." She looked at Isabella and smiled.

Lilac looked down at her daughter and said, "Go ahead, Isabella. Go outside. Don't stray. Stay close by."

In a flash, Isabella jumped up and ran outside with the rag doll dangling from her fingertips. She sat on the top step of the front porch, looking curiously at the dirty ragdoll. "Are you alright, doll? You look very sick and sad," she said, touching the dirty, once-white face with black stitched eyes and a red line of thread for a sad mouth. She pulled the three strands of its brown yarn hair. The doll was draped in a burlap dress with a black string around the waist and dirty brown finger marks all over. "You're dirty in your belly. I'm going to clean you."

Isabella walked down the steps carefully and made her way to the creek bank. She pushed aside some pebbles on the edge and knelt in the dirt. When she tried to dip the doll in the water, the three strings of yarn hair barely reached, so she adjusted her hold farther down the doll's legs. Then she leaned closer and immersed the entire doll in the cold, cascading water before losing her grip.

She stood and watched nervously as the doll got farther and farther away with every trickle of water falling from the higher level of rocks. She looked around anxiously for a long branch she could use to pull the doll back with, but found only pebbles around her. She imagined her mother's screaming when she found Carmile's doll soaked. She ran to the trees by the cottage and pulled on the first branch she could reach, then ran back to the creek. She carefully stepped on the wet pebbles and squatted, reaching as far as she could with the branch, but the doll had managed to travel too far away.

She lay down on the small, smooth rocks and squirmed farther over the edge, using her other hand to keep from falling into the water.

She reached the doll with the branch and pulled it to her, then let go of the stick and reached to grab the doll. Her hand slipped on the wet pebbles, sending her into the creek with a loud splashing sound. She popped up and grabbed the edge of the bank, her heart pounding fast and her little body shaking from the cold water, but her small hands slipped off the slippery pebbles.

Isabella no longer remembered the urgency of saving the doll or how mad her mother would be when she saw her dress was wet. She managed to get a hold of the bank's edge and pull herself up, but again slipped back in the water with another splashing sound. She grew more and more fearful that she might not get out and could drown. She began kicking her legs to stay above water as her little hands kept slipping on the smooth rocks on the bank.

She heard her name in the distance.

"Isabella! Isabella!" Lilac knelt on the edge of the creek and pulled her out, then held her close in her arms to warm her body.

"What were you thinking, Isabella?" Lilac said sternly.

"I wanted to clean the dolly, but she fell in the water. I'm sorry, Momma. I'm sorry."

Lilac shook her head in disbelief as she twisted Isabella's long hair to wring out the water. "Had I not heard the splash, you could have been dead! And… hopefully you will not catch a pneumonia from this… Oh dear," she said as she looked up to the sky.

Lilac walked Isabella back and sat her on the first step of the front porch where the sun's rays beamed. Carmile handed Lilac a green, hole-riddled, dirty old cotton blanket to wrap Isabella with.

"You are not to move from here!" Lilac said, pointing at the steps as she walked back inside, leaving the front door halfway open so she could check on her, as she felt Isabella's attention span was limited.

A flustered Lilac looked at Carmile, nodding her head in

embarrassment that Isabella had carried out such a senseless act. "This curse has removed all her ability to think intelligently."

Isabella quickly grew bored and snuck over to the door to peek in. She saw her mother sitting up straight and still with an orange rag wrapped around her head. On top of her head sat a small plate with a lit red candle. She was looking at Carmile, who was looking into a glass of dirty water. She put the glass to her mouth, uttered some words of a strange dialect, took a gulp, and spit it back in. Carmile looked eagerly into the glass, propping herself up, eyes widening. Her voice became deep and raspy as she chanted.

"Some say I can be evil,

But there is worse than me,

At the edge of the woods,

Dig and you shall see."

"Ha!" Carmile yelled cheerfully at discovering something of significance. "And that's where it is!"

"Where?" said Lilac. "What?"

With a mysterious expression on her face, Carmile replied, "The edge of the woods. That is where the curse is. I will dig it out, then all will be well. I will need Samuel to take me there at midnight on the 13th day following the next full moon."

"Yes, yes," Lilac replied, holding the plate over her head.

Carmile drew closer to Lilac and looked piercingly in her eyes. She softened her voice. "This will cost you much to do, but will cost you much, much more not to," she said as she turned and looked at Isabella.

Lilac gasped. "Whatever the cost. Isabella is growing sickly. Her luck is worsening, and I want my husband back."

"I will need twenty gold coins," Carmile said.

Lilac, shocked at the cost, nodded her head in agreement. "I will send it with Samuel on that night."

Smiling, Carmile said, "I will need it thirteen days before."

Isabella's heart sank. She knelt down and prayed just like she had seen Johndor do many times. She clasped her little hands together and looked up at the sky. "God, please don't let me be sick and ugly. Make me pretty and well."

Isabella heard the familiar sounds of the coach and saw Samuel off in the distance. She breathed a sigh of relief, then shouted, "Samuel is here! We have to leave now, Momma." She threw off the dirty blanket and ran toward the coach.

Carmile pointed to an altar hanging over the candle-ridden table. "Place the shillings for today's work there. Rest assured that it will all be done... no need to come back."

Lilac smiled gratefully at a stoic Carmile. "Thank you so much," Lilac said, bowing her head, then turning and exiting the ugly shack. She took a deep breath, relieved she did not have to return to that distasteful place.

"Your Majesty. Princess. Everything alright?" Samuel asked upon seeing Isabella soaked and a distracted Lilac quietly walking towards the coach, staring blankly ahead of her.

Lilac abruptly said to Samuel, "You are to assist Carmile on the 13th day after next full moon. Please consult Johndor, for he will know which day that is. See me precisely before you make your way there."

"As you say," Samuel said with a quick bow of the head.

"Do I have to come, Momma?"

"We need not come anymore." Lilac said. She dragged Isabella closer and gently pulled her wet hair up into a bun and patted the back of her wet dress dry, with her arms leaving her sleeves.

Isabella smiled and embraced her mother's wet arm for a quick second, then let go before her mother could shake her off.

Chapter 17

Ten years passed, and Lilac became a more frustrated and jaded queen, but she had never given up on her husband returning, or on her efforts to break the terrible curse that she thought plagued her daughter.

Isabella had suffered severe infections that kept her confined to bed for weeks at a time most of her life. Nightmares produced fears so deep she refused to sleep for days. Her greatest suffering was the boredom she endured inside the walls of the castle. She often banged her head against the walls out of loneliness and depression.

Minna had grown ill through the years, suffering from a debilitating disease not familiar to doctors, requiring her to rest throughout the day. Now fifteen, Isabella looked forward to taking care of her favorite nanny and refused to leave her bedside while she rested during her bouts of fatigue. Isabella would lie next to Minna, holding her hand and tattling on all of Lilac's erratic instances. Teary-eyed, she would stare at Minna as she fell asleep, imagining how disheartening and boring life would be without her. She would hug Minna gently until the crushing feeling dissipated.

Lilac, always afraid Isabella would catch some other ailment, only allowed her daughter limited time around Minna. She had grown obsessively scrupulous, demanding constant sterilization of all eating utensils, often separating plates, cups, and silverware for Isabella's and her own use.

This obsession of Lilac's irritated Bethlynn. In her bitterness over the lost promise Carmile had made all those years before, the queen had lost her last bit of politeness as well. Bethlynn became less reserved as time went by and her patience grew thinner. Lauren no longer lived in the castle, so Bethlynn had to care for Isabella and Lilac, plus see to Minna and her chores when she was ill.

Lilac had hired the help of an elite private tutor, feeling Isabella's inability to keep focused and her difficulty in understanding arithmetic required special attention. She was often heard saying the cursed spell had made Isabella unintelligent. Unfortunately, the royal reserves had grown low as Lilac did her best to restore Fleurham and was unable to retain the tutor's help.

Lauren and the tutor, Rolf Engleton, had fallen foolishly in love. They were married only months later in the castle chapel, then moved to the tiny town of Opal Lake, where Rolf cared for his elderly mother. Opal Lake's waters resembled the semi-precious stone in its name, with its glasslike reflection and glittery hues. It was in the most northern part of Kingsland, taking a good four hours from Fleurham by coach.

Lauren visited Minna religiously every Saturday and assisted Bethlynn with the chores, staying the night by Minna's side, then returning home on Sunday afternoon.

This Saturday in May would be special. Not only was it Minna's 70th birthday, with Thumbeline expected to pay a visit to her youngest sister, but it would also be only Thumbeline's second visit to the castle in 13 years. Johndor and Samuel constructed a ramp made of wooden planks so Thumbeline could easily access the castle's entrance, then both jumped in the coach and headed to fetch her. Johndor went along with Samuel to assist him with Thumbeline and to catch her up on the castle's affairs before she arrived.

Five hours later, laughter was heard outside the castle walls. The atmosphere had magically changed with Thumbeline's arrival. Samuel stopped the coach close to the ramp and carefully pulled the wheelchair out first and set it on the ground. Johndor and Samuel then took hold of Thumbeline's arms and legs and carried her out of the coach.

"Be careful with me. I am made of glass," Thumbeline said, laughing. Her head was cocked back, her pipe dangling from her toothless mouth.

"This is one dusty glass," Johndor said, laughing as they set her slowly into her chair. Samuel began to push the chair up the ramp.

"Not so fast. Let me take it all in," the 80-year-old mystic said, looking around at the royal grounds. She'd been expecting to see grand improvements to the castle and grounds, but it looked no better than it had 13 years earlier.

"Johndor was right," she said to herself quietly. "Not quite the kingdom, yet, still royal... still royal." She flared her nostrils and took a slow, deep breath, as if inhaling royal air. She tapped the wooden arms of her chair twice, signaling she was ready to be pushed inside.

Bethlynn and Lauren waited anxiously for Thumbeline at the entrance. Lauren smoothed the skirt of her mustard-colored dress and checked the golden bun that was wrapped tightly on her head, then clasped her hands together anxiously. Bethlynn adjusted the silver cord around her tiny waist and tucked a lock of her jet-black hair through the light blue silk hair bow she had sewn to match her dress. Her face flushed pink from the heat and her excitement at seeing Thumbeline in the castle after 13 years.

Johndor rushed ahead of Thumbeline to check the tea, scones, and cucumber sandwiches were prepared.

Lilac stood outside Isabella's room, arms crossed, listening to her daughter yell through her locked door.

"My hips hurt, Lilac! I don't think I can walk right now!"

"I am your mother! Do not call me by my name!" Lilac yelled back.

"When you feel like a mother to me, I will refer to you as Mother. Until then, you are Lilac!"

Lilac's nose crinkled in anger. She pushed her lips close to the door and said sternly, "You are to wear the pink dress with the lace neck. And do please try to look somewhat pretty today!"

"I will not! I am not a little girl any more... and I hate pink. You wear it if you like it so much!" Isabella stuck her tongue out toward the door. "And I cannot make myself pretty... I look like you!"

Lilac walked away, leaving Isabella to the special blend of tea Johndor made her every month during her moon cycle. Isabella had been a bit rebellious of late, mostly with her mother. She daydreamed of the day she would fall in love like Lauren and be whisked away from her mother's mean and obsessively superstitious behavior.

Isabella stared at the door, listening to make sure Lilac had gone. She lifted up her pillow and pulled out a special letter she'd made for Minna's birthday. She had decorated the letter with perfect ink hearts and a leaf she had found in the shape of a heart, which she asked Bethlynn to help her sew on.

"Dear Queeny,

You say one day I will be your queen,

but you are and will always be my queen,

my Queeny.

I wish I could make you get well.

I love you with all my heart.

Happy Birthday, Queeny!"

She kissed the letter and folded it in half, then stood in front of the mirror and tried to brush the wrinkles out of her sleeping gown.

She walked out and made her way down the hall to Minna's room.

Holding a tray with cucumber sandwiches, Johndor stopped in his tracks at the sight of Isabella and stared at her. "I will pay you a pence if you brush your hair," he said sternly, yet lovingly.

"And a scone too?" she said with a laugh. She turned back quickly, changed into her favorite red dress, and brushed her long, golden brassy colored hair.

Downstairs, Bethlynn was growing weary in the hot sun as she watched Thumbeline being pushed up the long ramp at the pace of a wedding procession. The kindly old woman waved and Bethlynn waved back, smiling. From behind her stiff smile, she muttered, "Please do hurry before I melt."

Thumbeline slapped the arms of her chair, and Samuel stopped. "I have forgotten the flowers in the coach." Samuel began to back Thumbeline's wheelchair up.

Bethlynn gasped in disbelief. She threw up her hands and went inside the castle, leaving Lauren with her untiring smile.

Bethlynn stood in the foyer fanning herself when she saw Isabella down the hall in her red dress. "Where is the pink dress I made you?"

"It's for little girls," Isabella said. "Please do not take any more dress orders from Lilac."

Bethlynn frowned. "As you wish, Isabella, but you must not call your mother by her name. We have discussed this many times now."

"She's not my real mother. I was adopted. My real parents were probably peasants who couldn't afford to raise me," Isabella said in a very serious tone, as if she believed it.

Bethlynn replied, "Well, not too far from a true story I know of."

"What?" Isabella exclaimed loudly.

"Oh, nothing. Did I say something?" Bethlynn said sarcastically as she walked away.

The front door swung open and Thumbeline entered, with Lauren pushing her. Their dresses matched, Thumbeline's a slightly lighter tone of gold with red flowers on the corset.

Lilac stepped out of the kitchen and smiled, pleased to see Thumbeline.

Thumbeline held Bethlynn's waist and beamed with joy as she said, "The most beautiful niece I have! She's like a porcelain doll."

Lauren quickly jumped up. "And me?"

Thumbeline held Lauren's hand. "You are beautiful too, but Bethy is beautifulest." "Happily, happily married I see." She gently patted Lauren's belly. "A boy."

Lauren giggled. Bethlynn leaned down close to Thumbeline. "And he will be ugly like his mother, because I am beautifulest," she said, laughing.

Everyone laughed, even Minna, who could overhear the conversation from the sitting room.

Thumbeline's smile subsided as she rubbed Lauren's belly gently. "There will be more... worry not," she said, feeling the unborn child might not survive.

Bethlynn took over pushing Thumbeline's chair so Lauren didn't exert herself now that it was known she was with child. Lauren walked beside Thumbeline into the sitting room, and Bethlynn parked her chair next to Minna, who was sitting on a large, sky-blue velvet settee.

Thumbeline reached for Minna's hand, and looked her in the eyes. "You can't complain. I took a trip just for you." Thumbeline looked around the room at Bethlynn standing next to her, Lauren standing behind Minna, patting her head, and Lilac and Johndor sitting on the settee across from them.

Johndor's smile faded when he noticed Thumbeline looked like she was about to cry.

Isabella walked into the sitting room slowly, looking down and fidgeting her fingers over a small envelope she was holding.

Thumbeline spotted her and flinched in surprise at how the little girl had grown. "Oh, beautiful princess. Come, let me kiss your beautiful face," she said, gesturing for the girl to come closer.

Isabella walked to Thumbeline, bumping into the tea table on her way there. She quickly looked at Lilac, who was shaking her head in disappointment, and held her breath. She reached Thumbeline and leaned down. Thumbeline touched Isabella's hair, then her face, her abdomen, and lastly, her hips. She gave her a gentle push toward Minna as she noticed the decorated letter in her hands.

Isabella sat on the floor in front of Minna. She fixed Minna's crooked right sock and pulled the edge of her lacy white cotton skirt from where she had sat on. She wrapped the skirt around Minna's legs to keep them warm, then caressed her feet.

Samuel stood at the door holding the flowers Thumbeline had brought. Lilac gestured for him to come in. Thumbeline took the flowers from Samuel and looked at Minna. "Have you met my new husband?" Thumbeline said jokingly, knowing from private confessions with Samuel, that there was not a chance in the world he would marry in this lifetime. Isabella laughed, but remained somewhat confused by the jest.

Thumbeline handed the gardenias to Minna, who smiled and took a sniff.

Minna started coughing, then looked at Isabella and said feebly, "These are for us two, Isabella."

Isabella nodded in acceptance of sharing the beautiful gardenia flowers. She smiled and held out her letter for Minna with both hands. A sadness came over her. She knew there was something very wrong with Minna. Her skin sagged from her frail bones, her burgundy hair was gray and scraggly, and her vivacious body had become fragile.

Although Minna displayed a fixed smile, Isabella knew her spirit was weak and afraid. Unable to contain her emotions, Isabella handed Minna the letter and walked out quickly, afraid someone would notice her tears. Overtaken by emotion, she ran out of the castle and into the woods, holding her stomach. She spotted her favorite tree, the shortest one, and collapsed, hugging it and sobbing.

"Please don't let her die. Please, please."

No one ran after Isabella this time. Everyone knew, including Minna.

As Bethlynn and Lauren served tea and scones to the queen and Minna and Thumbeline, Lilac checked the bottom of her teacup for the special chip in the porcelain to reassure her it was her private teacup.

Bethlynn offered Thumbeline a scone for the second time. Thumbeline did not even acknowledge Bethlynn, but instead turned to Queen Lilac and asked, "May I please spend the night with my sister, alone?"

Lilac replied, "No need to ask, Thumbeline. Anything you'd like is granted."

Lauren stood behind Minna and brushed her hair with her hands, then pulled it back with a green bow. She kissed Minna's head, then a tear threatened to fall, so she quickly drew her handkerchief to her face.

"Bethlynn, would you get me a glass of cold water?" said Thumbeline. Bethlynn nodded and jumped up to go to the kitchen.

Thumbeline watched her walk out, then whispered, "Is she still waiting for him?" Everyone nodded yes simultaneously without speaking a word, afraid Bethlynn might hear. She could have a raging temper occasionally.

Thumbeline shook her head in despair. "Fifteen good years wasted. My, my."

Bethlynn returned with a glass of water and set it on the table next to Thumbeline.

Thumbeline rubbed her sore knees and looked at Lilac. "Why is

Isabella so angry?"

Bethlynn quickly declared, "Because she hates her mother." Thumbeline stared at Lilac, waiting for a response.

Lauren said, "She's upset because she doesn't get out much, now does she?"

Lilac glared at Bethlynn and sighed, then looked back at Thumbeline. "I don't want harm to come to her. She is a magnet for accidents, illnesses, and just bad luck. I am afraid she will ruin the spell-cure that was done which hasn't fully taken effect yet."

No one had noticed Isabella standing discreetly by the door listening. *No wonder I have led such an unhappy life,* she thought, *feeling disillusioned and defeated, having believed the curse had been removed by the old witch Carmile.*

Minna took a deep breath to gather the strength to speak. "My princess is upset over a boy." Johndor clicked his tongue in disappointment and disbelief.

Rushing in, Isabella gestured for Minna not to say anything. She was embarrassed and shy in matters of love and female subjects, and only confided in Minna. Lilac had become angry when it was time for Isabella, whose body was changing, to wear a bustier, to say nothing of her shrieks when Isabella notified her that she'd bled for the first time when she was eleven. Lilac had a way of making Isabella feel ashamed of her femininity.

Isabella headed back to her room, hoping the subject would be dropped if she was not present.

Ever maternal in her love for the princess and her sister and nieces, Thumbeline wanted to know more so she could advise them. "Who is this boy?" she asked Minna very seriously.

"She is just spoiled," Lilac muttered.

Thumbeline cast a sideways glance at the queen and continued her questioning. "If it is important to her, then it is important to me."

Bethlynn leaned forward in her chair and spoke in a hushed tone. "Orlette, the jewelry maker, was interested in purchasing some of the queen's jewels. Her nephew William accompanied her for security reasons. While Lilac dealt with Orlette, William and Isabella carried on conversations about planets and stars and other cosmic nonsense. I remember at times they spent hours talking about the fateful day of the cursed arrow and the spell that crushed any chance of her happiness. The boy, just a bit older than Isabella, was mesmerized by the scar on her leg and how precise the triangular indention is."

Lauren cut in, "Her eyes lit up at the sound of his raspy voice. He called her China Doll, seeing she was so fragile and easily broken." A romantic Lauren smiled, as if she had been love-struck just speaking about it.

Minna turned to Thumbeline very slowly. "William was going to teach her to ride his horse. He was a bit reluctant. He was afraid her bad luck would cause her to fall, yet he wanted to take the chance if it meant spending some time with her."

Minna took a deep breath and coughed twice into her hands, then continued. "They agreed to meet in the woods, just on the edge, by the path. Isabella became afraid she would be seen and punished. She waited for all the king's men to leave, but by the time she arrived, he was not there. She never knew if he grew tired of waiting or never came at all. She was brokenhearted. William was her Prince Charming."

Thumbeline closed her eyes and, with the softest of tones, uttered the word "love." She rubbed her hands together, and under her breath said, "A love so true and pure... now that is the unfathomable cure."

Thumbeline held Minna's hands in hers and smiled. Still looking at Minna, she said to everyone else, "May I please have some time alone with my sister now?"

Everyone walked out quietly, sadness taking up residence on their faces once again.

Minna smiled and fixed her gaze on Thumbeline's beady eyes, her pounding heart filled with fear and grief. Tears fell onto Minna's pale cheek. She knew the end of her life had come, here and now.

Chapter 18

Bethlynn and Lauren rose early the next morning to see Thumbeline off. The two ladies waved farewell from the entrance of the castle. Thumbeline stuck her hand out of the curtain and waved back. Rolf, Lauren's husband, was due to arrive with the physician to examine Minna early that day. Lauren went back into the kitchen and grabbed a bowl of warm water she had prepared for Minna. She walked into the small room on the bottom floor that Lilac had set up for Minna and Johndor in the main house since Minna had fallen ill.

Lauren placed the bowl of water with floating mint and lavender leaves and two small cotton rags at the foot of Minna's bed, then moved to Minna's side and kissed her on the side of her head. "I'm going to wash you like a baby," she said, smiling into Minna's eyes.

Minna's eyes were dark and sunken, and she could barely lift the corners of her mouth in a smile for Lauren. Lauren moved to wring out a rag and put a dry one over her shoulder, ready to dry Minna quickly. She started at Minna's face, delicately wiping and drying.

The door slowly creaked open and Isabella stepped in, but waited by the door for Lauren to finish. Minna managed to lift her head to see who had come in, and Isabella flashed a big toothy smile and waved rapidly.

Minna tried to smile and lifted her hand inches off the bed, moving her fingers back and forth to invite the princess closer. Isabella curled up next to Minna, their heads touching, then lightly kissed Minna's cheek and held her hands.

Lauren finished up just as voices arrived outside the door.

"Isabella, please help me get Minna up and walk her to the sitting room," Lauren said nervously, as she heard the voices drawing nearer.

Isabella jumped to her feet, and put her hands behind Minna's neck and upper back. "Come on my Queeny. Oopsie daisy," she said, pushing her up gently until she was sitting.

Lauren slid Minna to the edge of the bed as Isabella held her up. Isabella wrapped Minna's right arm around her neck, Lauren took hold of the other arm, and together, they very slowly pulled her up.

Minna stood and stared at the wall in front of her, trying to fit her face in the oval gilded mirror hanging in front of her. The movement made Minna lose her balance and she plopped back on the bed, pulling Lauren and Isabella with her. The three laughed as they fell to the bed together. Lauren and Isabella lifted Minna up again and took three small steps towards the door. Lauren noticed that Minna was much weaker than the day before, and began to turn her back toward the bed, causing Minna to lose her balance again.

The two ladies nervously shouted out for help.

Rolf, who had been waiting in the sitting room with the physician, ran quickly to Minna and carried her back to her bed.

Isabella, panting, her heart beating fast, stood next to the bed, trying to hold Minna's hand.

Rolf softly rubbed his hand back and forth over Lauren's abdomen. "Are you alright, darling?"

Lauren nodded yes and rubbed her nose, sniffling, trying not to cry. She leaned her head against his chest and sobbed.

Bethlynn arrived with a tray of tea and nervously set the cups out on the little round table next to Minna's bed. Holding her breath for periods of time, she stared at Minna.

The physician stepped around Lauren, who was standing by the bed, holding Minna's hand. "Dr. Tottle at your service."

Isabella sat on the bed next to Minna and stared at her eyes. They were dimmer, having lost their last bit of glimmer. Her eyelids were heavy and her face grayish, with no sign of substance left in her spirit. Minna looked up at Isabella and tried to speak, but only managed a crackly, feeble sound through her half-open mouth. "Help me, help me..."

Isabella's chest trembled with short breaths, a prelude to quiet, yet forceful tears as she felt her heart breaking. She believed she had failed Minna.

Just as Dr. Tottle gestured, waving his hand at Isabella to give Minna some space, a frenzied Lilac burst into the room. The queen, embarrassed that Dr. Tottle had to ask Isabella to get off the bed, headed straight for the princess, waving her arms around and yelling, "Isabella, Minna is very sick... please go to your room and get in your dress right now!"

A saddened Johndor, who was standing by Isabella, helped the startled girl off the bed. Paralyzed by emotions, Isabella stood dazed, still holding Johndor's hand.

"Go!" Lilac pointed at the door.

Rolf, who was standing by the door, held the doorknob tight to stop the door from slamming after Isabella swung it as hard as she could.

She ran crying to her room, slammed the door, and locked it behind her. She threw herself on the bed and curled up in the fetal position, sobbing.

Lilac checked the door, reassuring herself Isabella had not come back in. She then ran to Minna and grasped her hands tightly. "I know. I always knew... I love you, Mother."

Minna's eyes blinked with relief and she squeezed Lilac's hands faintly. Her gaze found Johndor standing on her other side, across from Dr. Tottle, his eyes glazed with tears not strong enough to fall. Johndor smiled and placed his bony hands on Minna's forehead, softly patting her face. She smiled back ever so sweetly, her eyes lighting up for half a second, then she took a deep breath and her pains ceased. Her body became numb. She let her eyes close, slipping into the dreaded eternal sleep.

Bethlynn and Lauren hugged Lilac, with a sense of relief over the long-kept secret. The three whimpered gently, cuddled in each other's arms.

Thumbeline yelled up to Samuel, "Stop, Samuel! Stop!" and banged on the roof of the coach. Her chin dropped, and she took a long breath, then pulled open the side curtain and looked up at the sky. A snow-white dove soared up high above them. She wiped a tear from her face, knowing in her heart her sister had left the earthly plane. She made the sign of the cross on her body with the rosary she had been praying with since leaving the castle grounds and banged on the coach again. The coach lurched forward, and Thumbeline continued praying. "Hail Mary, full of grace…"

The mood was solemn throughout the castle. There was a feeling of emptiness… of something missing, a feeling that an essence that was warm and loving was no longer there. Only the pain of a nurturing spirit no longer residing within its walls was present.

The physician offered his apologies for not being able to get there sooner. He offered to send a priest back from his hometown of Glastonshire, a quaint village just ten miles from Opal Lake.

"Yes, please. We would be most grateful," Lilac said.

Rolf embraced Lauren. "I will be back, darling." He turned to the physician and gestured toward the door. "Dr. Tottle, shall we?"

Dr. Tottle bowed to the queen and made his way toward the front doors, noticing the paintings of Maurice on the wall. Although Dr. Tottle had grown older and his memory was fading, he could not help but remember the familiar face of the strong, bearded man and his awkward situation when they first met in Nokbershire. Despite his professional respect for the privacy of all involved, he still could not help his curiosity. Stepping out the front doors of the castle, he asked Rolf, "What happened to the king?"

Rolf shrugged his shoulders. "Story has it, he went after an archer who shot a cursed arrow that hit the princess and unraveled a terrible spell... the reason for her terrible luck. He never came back. Nobody knows if he is dead or alive. He has yet to be found or heard from. In fact, Lauren believes Minna became sick after his disappearance."

"Was she that fond of him?" Dr. Tottle asked.

"Yes, and he of her as well, I hear," Rolf replied as he assisted Dr. Tottle onto the horse.

Dr. Tottle looked piercingly down at Rolf. "Then we shall inform him of Minna's passing."

Rolf stared at Dr. Tottle, shaking his head in confusion, then jumped on the horse.

"I will lead the way," Dr. Tottle said. "We must stay on this path, but pay very close attention when we reach Brothers' Cross. One wrong turn can lose you for a day, a month, a century... or forever."

Rolf directed his steed carefully for the elderly Dr. Tottle. He paid careful mind to details on the way, as getting lost was not an option. As he worried over not returning to see his child born or hold his lovely Lauren again, he began to wonder if that was what happened to King Maurice.

They rode for two hours before Dr. Tottle saw Brothers' Cross in the distance. Against the sky, he recognized the canopy of intertwining leaves and branches of four connecting trees. As Rolf listened intently, Dr. Tottle began to recount the story of how the crossing came to be named.

"Myth tells of four orphaned trickster brothers who using their striking resemblance fool and rob throughout the village. The townspeople gathered one evening after what would be the brothers' last gimmick, which led to the accidental death of the clergyman and decided the brothers' fate. One night, as the old clergyman lay in his bed asleep, the brothers broke in to rob the donations from the town's church. The old man woke and ran staggering, chasing them barefoot into the dark woods. Unfortunately, he stepped on a sharp branch, fell, and hit his head on a tree stump, breaking his oil lamp. He landed on the lamp, and his sleeping gown quickly caught fire. Unconscious from the fall, the old man burned to death. The four brothers were hung from four branches of a great tree that stood in the center of the path where different trails divert, leading into different towns. They were buried in each of the four corners, and that same night, the great tree mysteriously burned to the ground. Some say it was the ghost of the clergyman."

Dr. Tottle put his hand on Rolf's shoulder as they reached the crossing. Rolf pulled the reins and they stopped. The doctor looked down at the path, but felt the horse begin to turn, then shouted, "Do not let him turn! We will lose our direction. The Brothers' Cross is said to be haunted by the brothers, tricking travelers to lose their way."

The old man scratched his head, trying to figure out which path to direct Rolf on. They had taken one path to get them where they were, so there were three options left.

A gentle flapping came from the branches of a tree as three leaves fluttered to the ground. A white dove appeared, then flew just above the path to the right.

"Follow the dove," Dr. Tottle said, smiling. He remembered that as a boy, his father always told him to watch for signs from above. He had made it a habit ever since to look up whenever he needed answers.

Trusting Dr. Tottle, Rolf confidently steered the horse down the right path. The dove soared higher and higher until it disappeared in the sky. The two men rode another two hours before they noticed the air become still and stale. The blue sky had progressively turned to shades of gray, and it smelled of rain. Dr. Tottle sighed in relief that he'd correctly chosen the path leading to the cottage where Maggy Mae and Maurice lived.

The entrance at the edge of the woods was blocked by ivy bushes, so the horse slowed down. Dr. Tottle pointed at Maggy Mae's cottage, saying, "Straight on through."

Rolf replied, "Seems quite blocked. Shall we attempt to cross it?"

"No harm. Only ivy," Dr. Tottle reassured him.

The horse slowly trotted, then stopped again right before the ivy web. He flapped his lips and neighed as he stepped backward. Rolf slapped the horse on his side, trying to force him forward. With an unimaginable quickness, as if possessed, the steed raised up on his hind legs, sending Dr. Tottle flying off, and he landed hard in the deep ivy entanglement. The horse jumped and lurched in all directions, neighing loudly while Rolf screamed for him to halt over and over again. All Rolf could do was hold on tight to the leather straps and squeeze his legs around the horse's ribs, holding on for dear life.

An assertive deep voice from the other side of the bushes told the horse to stop. A tall, robust man with salt-and-pepper hair and beard ran toward them with what Rolf thought was a very angry look on his face.

Rolf yelled nervously at the man, "I am Rolf! I come for Queen Lilac. King Maurice, is it you?"

"Yes! It is I," Maurice said, trying to recognize who this man on a wild horse might be.

"The doctor needs help!" Rolf said, panting as he fought to hold onto his out-of-control horse.

"What doctor?"

"Dr. Tottle! Right there on the ground before you," Rolf shouted, pointing into the ivy bush, three feet in front of Maurice.

Maurice stepped closer to find Dr. Tottle facedown and motionless. He quickly grabbed the doctor by the shoulder and turned him over. His face was too much to bear. Maurice let go quickly and looked up, bringing his hands up to cover his eyes. He took a deep breath and brought his hands to his waist, then looked at Rolf, still struggling with his horse. Maurice jumped over the ivy and Dr. Tottle and grabbed the leather strap around the horse's face.

"What's his name?" Maurice asked.

"Rupert!" Rolf yelled back.

Maurice laid his other hand on the horse's muzzle and drew its ear down so he could speak soothingly into it. "It's alright," he whispered. "It's alright. Stay still, Rupert. Stay still."

Rupert made one loud snort, scratched the gravel with his right hoof, then settled down and stood still. Rolf jumped off as Maurice tied Rupert to a nearby cedar tree. He ran to Dr. Tottle and broke the vines of ivy away from his body, then turned him over. Dr. Tottle's face was cherry red and swollen like a balloon, covered in welts. His eyes were wide open, his heart still, and his body lifeless and heavy.

Rolf turned away, trying to keep from being sick.

The two men pulled the doctor out of the ivy bushes to a spot Maurice had cleared of branches and rocks between two cedar trees. Rolf nearly hyperventilated as he paced around in hysterics, feeling guilty for the old physician's death.

"I don't know what possessed Rupert," he said, his voice breaking.

Maurice stood still as a statue, in a state of complete confusion and shock. With one hand on his hip and the other brushing his beard, he spoke very slowly as he said, "Did you say... Queen Lilac?"

Rolf, voice quivering, still in a state of nerves, replied. "I am husband to Lauren. We are here... I am here... to deliver the news that Minna passed at sunrise this morning."

Maurice jerked up straight as a soldier on call. Shaking his head from side to side, his eyes filled with tears. "Was it sudden?" he asked, as memories from his last days at the castle flashed in his mind.

"I'm afraid not. She had been suffering from an unusual illness for some time now," Rolf replied.

Maurice's heart woke and throbbed with old pain. He fought his tears back as he looked Rolf in his eyes, afraid of what he might say. "My daughter? My princess?"

"She is well," Rolf said, with a noticeably happier tone in his voice.

"Would you take me there?" Maurice begged.

"It would be an honor!" Rolf held his hand over his heart.

Maurice bent down over Dr. Tottle's body, holding his eyes shut. "In the name of the Father, the Son, and the Holy Ghost. Rest in peace." He started back to the house to inform Maggy Mae that he must leave for a time, but then turned and ran back to Rolf, clasping his hands, as if in prayer. "I beg you, do not leave without me. I beg of you."

"You have my word," Rolf said, bowing his head.

Maurice walked around the cottage in a daze to inform Maggy Mae. He left her with disapproving words in her mouth and rapidly walked to Rolf. Maggy Mae walked quickly behind him and stopped at the sight of Rolf. All Maurice thought about was his princess. Nothing else mattered to him at that moment. He mounted the horse behind Rolf. "Let's go," Maurice said assertively, ignoring a distressed Maggy Mae, frozen in shock mid-way between the cottage and the forest.

Maurice looked all around nervously, afraid of becoming lost.

He raised his voice above the sharp wind. "Are you sure this is the right way?"

Rolf kept his gaze locked straight forward as he replied, "We must get to Opal Lake to get to Glastonshire. We must inform Dr. Tottle's family. That route will take us to Fleurham."

Maurice had given up finding his way back to Fleurham after his first son was born. His desire to raise Isabella had never ceased in his heart, but he trusted she would be well taken care of as long as Johndor and Minna were at her service. In the back of his mind, he always worried about her. Through the years, he had become fraudulently enamored with Maggy Mae, as she continued to concoct spell-binding teas to assure his fidelity to her, but on that day, the grief he felt in his heart over Minna's passing woke him out of the trance.

Chapter 19

The midday sun beat down on both men as they waited for Dr. Tottle's wife to respond to their relentless knocking. Maurice, thirsty, tired, and still in a state of disbelief, pushed the door open. There sat a frail, thin old lady draped in a dark gray wool blanket, on a wooden bench, staring at a fireless bed of coals.

"Madame... Madame!" Rolf called to her from the doorway.

The old woman didn't budge.

They took the liberty of entering while announcing themselves so as not to startle the old woman. They moved around to address her from the front, but she remained motionless except her two pointer fingers, which were fidgeting with a strand of golden silk string.

Rolf knelt down to make eye contact with her. "Mrs. Tottle?" She began to rock back and forth, showing no recognition of the fact that there were two men standing before her.

Maurice and Rolf walked outside. A man with long gray hair framing his bony face and dressed in a brown, patched-up coat, was leaning on a tree at the edge of the Tottle property. "She's not all there, you know," he said in a thick country accent.

"Mrs. Tottle, you mean?" Rolf said.

117

"Yeah," the stranger replied. "Not since she tried to give birth fifty years ago. It was either the baby or her, they say. They also say—"

"Has he any other relatives?" Maurice asked.

"Only people that knock on his door are sick or have a sick someone that needs care." The stranger scratched his head and took a step forward. "I suspect something's gone wrong with the, uh... old doctor, eh?"

The man used a long, thick wooden tree branch for a walking stick as he walked toward the two men, leaning on the stick every few steps. His heavy boots made a stomping, crunching sound over the leaves. He held out his hand as he neared Maurice and Rolf. "Name's Roland."

"Rolf, from Opal Lake."

"Maurice, from Fleurham."

The men shook Roland's hand, suspicious of his unexpected, awkward appearance. They were unable to keep from staring at his left eye, which had no pupil. The yellow glossy ball residing in the socket was most disturbing.

Rolf and Maurice looked at each other, then Maurice turned to the strange man and said, "The good doctor has had an accident and died."

Roland cocked his head to the side in surprise.

"We would like to bring his body back to his town," Rolf said.

Roland laughed. "I can do that job for a small price. I'm the one who picks up the pieces around here when things get broken."

The two men nodded their heads in relief.

"Whereabouts is the good doctor?" Roland said.

Rolf replied, "Nokbershire. After the last village, west about seven miles... end of the woods' edge."

"Hmm," Roland replied. "After the last village, then west, you say? That sounds like the witch's shack right there."

Maurice tensed and paid close attention to the man.

Roland continued, "You know about the evil witch, don't you?

Name's Marguarite, they call her 'the silver witch.' She was born with silver hair... teased all her life, even by her own mother. They say that's why she turned evil. They found the farthest town away from all people and hid her there. Wonder whatever happened to that ol' witch anyway?"

Perturbed by that information, Maurice shook his head. Somehow things began to make sense. His entire life had changed in a matter of hours that day so many years ago. *I have been living a lie!* he thought.

Roland startled Maurice out of his blank stare. "Well, is that where the old doctor is? Did she get him too?"

"She no longer lives there. The doctor's body lies at the edge of the path."

Roland held his hand out, palm up. "Well, I'm not scared of any witch. It's the act of being scared that will get the best of you."

Maurice reached into his thick leather vest, then dropped five coins into Roland's hand. Roland quickly closed his hand. "I'll see to it that the good doctor receives a well-deserved burial." Roland held out his other hand, as if about to receive something more. "Now... you two didn't kill him, correct?"

Maurice dropped two more coins in Roland's grungy palm. Roland bowed his head. "Good day, gentlemen." He walked off, crushing the leaves under his big boots with every step, and disappeared behind the wide tree he came from.

The men made their way to fetch the priest and head back to Fleurham.

Chapter 20

An anxious Lauren fiddled around with her wet tissue, folding it in different shapes as the hours passed and Rolf did not make it back. The day's light had begun to fade. The three ladies sat in the kitchen as Johndor made linden tea to calm their angst over deciding who would be best to inform Isabella of Minna's passing. It was a day they had all dreaded for Isabella.

Still angry with her mother for forcing her out of Minna's room, Isabella lay in her bed, humming her favorite song. She hugged her silver silk pillow to her face and traced the beveled trim edge of her nightstand with her index finger. She stopped humming when a gentle knock sounded on her door.

"It's Bethlynn."

"Come," Isabella said.

Bethlynn entered and sat on the bed, propping Isabella's legs over her lap and stroking them gently through her silky, burgundy nightgown.

"Isabella, Minna no longer suffers. She is now in heaven."

Isabella leaped forward, throwing her arms over Belthlynn's neck, and began to sob on her chest. Bethlynn rocked the princess back and forth as she cried on her bosom. Bethlynn ran her fingers through Isabella's hair gently to calm her, shedding her own quiet tears. They comforted each other. Bethlynn always came across as hardened by life, but her heart was sweet, compassionate, and selfless, and Isabella loved her dearly.

Bethlynn wiped Isabella's face with her handkerchief, fixed her hair away from her face, and walked her downstairs, where she sat with Johndor, not letting his hand go for a single second. Both sat patiently on a blue velvet settee near the foyer of the castle. Isabella's eyes were swollen, her nose pink, and her eyebrows were scrunched in anger at Lilac.

Johndor looked at Isabella every so often and smiled as if everything was alright with him, but he was heartbroken. The only words he spoke were "poor soul," over and over again.

Isabella looked at Johndor, wanting to tell him that it was okay to cry.

Samuel opened the front door and announced he could see Rolf and the priest from a distance. Lauren stepped outside to wait for her husband. The two horses drew in closer, she saw a man dressed all in black atop a large gray horse. As the horses got closer, she saw a third person wave his arm from behind her husband. Lauren walked toward the men to get a closer look.

"Do my eyes deceive me?" she said. "That looks like Maurice."

Rolf waved at Lauren from afar. Consumed with emotion at the possibility that the man might be Maurice, Lauren did not acknowledge Rolf. She couldn't believe what she was seeing. The closer they got and the more she noticed of the man—his smile, his hair, his posture, the more she was indeed sure it was Maurice.

She clapped her hand over her mouth and rushed back to the castle. She slung the door open and yelled, "It is Maurice! He is here!"

Lilac popped straight up from her chair and gasped, trembling, with her hand to her mouth. Johndor held Isabella's hand tighter as she sat up in excitement. Johndor would always come first before any man for Isabella, even her own father. She wondered if he held her hand tighter because he needed her right now or because he didn't want her to run to a man who hadn't found his way back to her for all these years.

Lauren's smile turned into a frown at everyone's reaction. She was expecting excitement, and instead there was unmoved anger and apathy. Bethlynn's sadness over Minna was too deep for her to pay any mind to anything else. She sat in the kitchen, emotionless, and slowly sipped her tea, staring at the wall across from her, where Minna's white apron hung.

The three men walked towards the entrance. Maurice tread a little more quickly, his heart racing with joy at seeing Isabella and nervousness at seeing Lilac. The priest and Maurice entered and stood in the foyer, still and speechless, understanding a myriad of mixed emotions were to be expected. Maurice nervously touched Lilac on the shoulder. Lilac flinched, bumping the large gilded golden mirror above the foyer table with her shoulder.

"I am sorry, Lilac."

Stoically, the queen just looked at him as if she were looking at a ghost. Was he sorry because Minna had passed or because he never came back? Her heart fluttered with emotions... anger, love, hope. She wanted to hug him, but she was frozen in overwhelming confusion.

The king appraised his wife, feeling pity for how time had not been on her side. He grasped Johndor's shoulder and looked in his eyes. "My heart is with you in your time of grief, Johndor."

Johndor brought Isabella's hands to Maurice's.

"Your father. Isabella, greet him with a hug."

Isabella stood nervously and gave the bearded man a hug, looking for Lilac's approval or punishment.

"You are a woman! A beautiful woman," he said. She smiled, feeling good to be called a beautiful woman.

Maurice stood nervously, looking around the inside of the castle and from Lilac to Johndor as he said, "May I please be present for the services?"

Lilac took a deep breath. Isabella gulped nervously, hoping her mother would approve his request. She wanted to get to know her father, regardless of what had happened. She'd had an innate admiration for him since she was small.

Lilac looked at Johndor for an answer. Johndor nodded yes, knowing Minna had loved Maurice like one of her own. In his heart of hearts, he grieved that Minna did not live to see Maurice return and had died not knowing if he was alive or dead. Or perhaps, her secret last wish, if those did in fact exist, had been for Maurice's safe return. Johndor stood up and walked to the kitchen to prepare scones and tea.

Isabella grabbed Johndor's hand to walk with him. He turned to the princess and said, "Stay with your father, he would like to be with you."

"But I can help you prepare," she said.

"Go, Isabella. It has been 10 years since you've seen him. Bethlynn will be with you." He shouted to Bethlynn, snapping her out of her gloom. She shook her head and scurried out, wiping her tears.

Isabella hugged Johndor and walked away with Bethlynn, holding her hand and drying her tears with the other.

"Now is not the right time, but I will explain," Maurice told everyone standing around him. "For now, I would like to know what happened to Minna."

Rolf cleared his throat, gaining everyone's attention. He gestured for the priest to step forward and present himself.

The priest stepped inside and greeted everyone with a cordial smile and a bow of his head. "Father Stephen Marbone," he said as he adjusted his long black cassock. "My deepest sympathies."

Bethlynn released Isabella's hand and ushered her toward the kitchen, then led Father Marbone and the rest to the small chapel. The sun had set and twilight shaded the sky with a lavender sheet, thinning the last of the light peeping in through the mosaic chapel windows.

Johndor and Isabella sat in the kitchen, staring glumly into their teacups while the others were gathered in the chapel, talking about Minna's last days and final arrangements. In the days leading up to the inevitable, she and Johndor had told their daughters her body was to be buried in Cuvington, where they had lived, married, and birthed them, two and a half hours north of Fleurham. Although most of the town had burned down during the Revolt of 1553, Johndor had promised Minna that one day he would take her back home.

Chapter 21

Cuvington was never fully rebuilt, but some structures still stood, including the castle walls where Queen Catriona, who had eventually raised Lilac as her own and leaving her heir, ruled. She was called the Snow Queen for her pale skin, white as snow. Every gown she wore was pure white and adorned in silver trim, and her eyes where the most beautiful crystal blue.

Johndor was a trained archer who had won many championships for the castle. He was renowned as a man of short stature yet strong character, compassionate and wise beyond his 35 years. He and his pregnant wife Minna lived in Cuvington with their two daughters when the French invaded in 1553, taking jewels, gold, even family members. Like many other residents of Cuvington, Johndor and Minna were left destitute, hardly able to feed their two girls or care properly for Minna and the baby on the way.

After the French left, Johndor's daily mission became finding work. One cold fall morning, he was walking along the path toward the town of Furough Wells, which the townsmen were attempting to reconstruct. Like putting together a puzzle, Johndor tried to fit loose bricks into the missing gaps in the path, which had broken away during the revolt. He gathered old pieces of wood and burnt items from the ground and piled them together for easy discard when a horse and wagon approached from the castle.

The driver recognized Johndor and stopped the wagon. "Well if it isn't Robin Hood himself. Get yourself in the cart before you freeze. Got some sacks to keep you warm back there. Where are you headed to?"

"Looking for some work, sir," Johndor said, trying to smile warmly, tasting the bitterness as he gently swallowed his pride.

"What kind of work?"

Johndor replied, "Whatever is offered to me. No time to fuss. Got a wife and two daughters to feed. And another on the way."

"Well I haven't any arrows to shoot, but you can help me deliver and unload these goods to the castle... Snow Queen's. But I'm afraid I've only got work for you for one day."

Johndor opened his eyes wide and laughed. He clapped his hands together, feeling like the luckiest man in the world. He jumped into the cart and pulled the empty burlap sacks around himself for warmth. "Thank you, sir. Thank you."

"The name's Charles Roberts," the butcher said as he started moving up the path again.

Upon arrival at the Snow Queen's castle, Johndor jumped from the cart, staring in awe at how close he was to the entrance of the brown brick structure. He had never been to anything but the fields outside the grounds during target archery competitions. From this close up, the castle seemed colossal to Johndor. He greeted everyone that crossed his path with a smile and a tip of his hat. He even greeted the queen when she exited the castle to get in her coach, knowing she probably wouldn't even notice him among all the workers. But he could have sworn she returned his greeting with a very slight nod of her head.

Johndor carried crate after crate of frozen poultry, bread, and ale to the storage room situated on the lower floor within the keep of the castle.

The castle was preparing for Queen Catriona's special dinner event with the French royals, to be held in hopes of finding a peaceful agreement.

"Last one, here you go," Charles the butcher said to Johndor as he passed him the last crate of ale. Johndor walked slowly back to the wagon, looking up and down at the castle. He swept his hand across the bricks to feel the cold, rough texture on his fingertips, knowing it would most likely be the last time he came this close to royalty. He jumped in the empty wagon, laid his tired body down and propped his head on a half-filled burlap sack. He smiled all the way back.

That afternoon, Johndor arrived home beaming. He kissed Minna on the cheek, and she rewarded him with a big kiss. Minna and the two girls gathered around him by the fireplace. The two girls jumped up and down in excitement at seeing his fists closed and a big smile on his face. Minna pulled a footstool under his heels as he sat on his favorite burgundy wooden leather armchair and the three girls took a seat on the floor, preparing to hear about his adventure. What he didn't know was that Minna stood watching him every morning until she would lose him in the distance. She'd seen him climb onto the butcher's cart that morning and thanked the heavens. He leaned forward and held his closed hands out, then opened one hand to Bethlynn and Lauren, both under the age of four. They each grabbed a caramel truffle, giggled, and popped them in their little mouths. He opened his other hand to Minna, revealing a third truffle and a day's pay. Minna took the truffle, nibbled off a piece, and hid the rest high on a shelf.

Johndor went outside and dragged in a potato sack, half filled with remnants Charles the butcher had let him have out of pity. Bread, potatoes, jam, cracked eggs in a jar, and a small piece of cheese. With the shillings he'd earned, he would buy a chicken.

That night he slept contentedly, knowing that his family's bellies were full and would be for a few more days. He rose early the next morning, anticipating another lucky day. He continued looking for work day after day for the next week, with no luck. On the eighth morning, Minna lay resting in bed, too hungry and weak to see her husband off. Worried about Minna, Johndor didn't search very far for work. He returned quickly to the cottage to tend to her and the children.

Later that day, with a loud knock on the cottage door, a voice called Johndor's name. He answered the door to find Charles the butcher. Johndor's eyes lit up at the hope that he might have more work.

"Johndor, my friend, you have been summoned."

"Summoned?" Johndor asked, startled.

"And by none other than the Snow Queen herself."

"The Q-Q-Queen? Can't be. You must have the wrong person. Surely she—"

Charles clapped Johndor on the shoulder and said, "Word has it she noticed your good work, but mostly your good will and spirit. I explained your troubles to her manservant..." He shrugged with a big smile, happy to see such a good man catching a break. "Let's not keep her waiting, shall we?"

Johndor turned to grab his cloak and hat, but hesitated when he saw Minna leaning weakly against the wall. Minna spoke before Johndor could get a word out. "Be on your way, Johndor. I will be just fine."

The Snow Queen sat on her throne, slightly slumped over and paler than a blanket of snow. Sadness emanated from her with every breath. Her white silk and velvet gown covered her from her chin to the very tip of her toes. Her ginger hair, thin and dry, poked out of her royal cape's hood, and she seemed to cling to the thick, heavy cape for warmth, though the castle was quite warm.

Johndor was tempted to examine her bottom eyelids and offer her an herbal concoction to aid her fatigued body. Yet he stayed quiet, smiling softly and praying silently, "God, have mercy on this sickly young woman."

The Snow Queen spoke delicately. "Your presence is greatly appreciated."

Johndor bowed his head. "The honor is all mine, Your Majesty."

The queen took a deep breath, then said, "I understand your family has been left stripped and destitute from the ungodly aftermath of the revolt."

"Yes, my lady."

"I have been told you have two daughters and a child on the way."

"Yes, my lady."

"How is your wife's health, Mr...."

"Johndor, my lady. Johndor Amridge," he said, bowing his head again. "My wife Minna suffers, my lady. We have not enough to feed the children, not to mention the poor soul trying to grow inside her. She fears it will die from malnutrition, my lady. I am filled with angst as well. Searching every day for any little job I can do to provide for my family."

The Snow Queen carefully sat up in her gilded throne, took another deep breath, then stood slowly and ushered the court away with her gloved hand. "What I am about to offer may sound cold and heartless, but I mean it with the best of intentions for your family, as well as for mine."

"I understand," Johndor said, nervously gripping his hat tighter in front of his waist.

"I have a condition, as did my mother before me. She no longer lives because of it. My illness has left me barren. Although no one dares to speak it, I do not have many years left. I must pass down the royal crown—the legacy cannot die with me."

Johndor gulped, wide-eyed.

"I can reward your family greatly for the rest of time, if only…" she looked down, gently clasped her hands together, and deeply inhaled a long breath of courage.

Johndor tensed, taking small sips of air to hide his uneasiness. He clenched his teeth, afraid of what would come out of her mouth next.

The Snow Queen took another quick breath and flared her nostrils. Her words gained strength as she spoke hastily. "I offer you the guarantee that your family will never be hungry again in return for your child to be."

Johndor's legs became weak. His face flushed red, and warmth crawled through his bones.

"Your family will live inside the annex houses on the compound. You will always have work, money, food, and a roof."

Johndor began to rock side to side on his feet, struggling with terrible guilt over the idea that the offer was somewhat enticing. *What a price to pay to ensure my family's survival,* he thought. What will this do to Minna? He looked at the queen with a blank expression.

Queen Catriona stepped down to face Johndor eye to eye, grasped his hands, and pulled them close to her chest. "You will lose that child one way or the other. I guarantee a wonderful life for it, and your family. I am dead inside, and soon will be dead outside. I will not have lived until I can have a child of my own."

Her sad eyes welled up with tears. She smiled and bowed her head as she exited, leaving Johndor alone until the manservant guided him out to where the queen's coach awaited to return him home.

Circumstances didn't leave Minna and Johndor a choice. They convinced themselves that they were blessed to have two daughters when the unlucky queen had none, and that the third child would actually be the luckiest. It would be a blessing in disguise.

Three months later, in the special quarters reserved for Minna to birth, a baby girl was born. Queen Catriona named her Lilac Charlotte and spent every waking hour with her, cherishing their time as if every day were her last... until her final day did indeed come.

On a warm day in August, Minna and Johndor inherited the care of three-year-old Lilac Charlotte and her royal ministry. Johndor and Minna had not missed one day of Lilac's life since her birth.

Chapter 22

As night fell in Fleurham, Bethlynn and Lauren prepared beds for Father Marbone and Maurice. Busywork helped them get through the overwhelming emotions of the day, though they felt awkward dressing a bed for the king in the annex house where the help lived.

Lauren held a pillow to her chest. "I feel wrong putting Maurice in this room. There is something just not right with all of this. Where has he been? Why didn't he come back before now?"

Bethlynn replied under her breath, "Just follow orders, Lauren. Just follow orders."

"Perhaps he can sleep in Isabella's room. And Isabella can sleep with her mother."

Bethlynn stopped tucking the sheet and looked at Lauren sharply. "Perhaps then there will be two people to bury tomorrow. I don't think Isabella will be very happy to sleep with her mother."

"Well, then, how about if she sleeps with you?" Lauren suggested.

Bethlynn gently pushed Lauren out the door. "You go ask Her Royal Highness. I certainly will not suggest such a thing."

Lauren stepped quickly back in the room. "Oh no, no. You do it. She listens more to you."

Bethlynn gently bopped Lauren over the head with the pillow and went to look for Lilac. As she crossed the great hall, she noticed two figures in the distance past the French doors leading to the courtyard. Bethlynn quietly opened the doors, hoping to catch their attention. She slowly walked closer to them, but Lilac—loudly demanding an explanation from Maurice—took no notice of Bethlynn. Lilac's anger made her nose scrunch up as if she was preparing to slap Maurice. Her head shook in frustration and her voice broke with emotion as she continuously knocked on his chest with her open hand. She had dutifully and hopefully waited year after year for the sweet return of her husband, which never came to pass. She'd grown numb with loneliness and grief, but her emotions began to surface as she finally faced her long-lost husband.

Maurice grasped her by the shoulder to ease her obvious anger. Her resentment began to melt. After all these years, she still desired him.

Bethlynn stepped forward, clearing her throat, then said, "Pardon, we would like to ask permission to place Maurice in Isabella's room."

Maurice moved his hand away from Lilac's shoulder quickly. Lilac replied, not taking her eyes off Maurice. "He may sleep in my quarters. I will move to Isabella's. Thank you, Bethlynn. Now leave us."

That was easy, Bethlynn thought as she left the courtyard.

Maurice brought his hand back up to Lilac's shoulder. "I am so—"

"Why did you leave us? When we needed you most!" Lilac yelled, holding back her tears and trembling with heartbreak.

"I left chasing the archer. I became lost in the woods, ending up in a place that would rob me of everything I had... of everything I was."

He continued to explain in detail.

"Isiah died and there was no way for me to leave. The forest was dense and disorienting and so unfamiliar that I lost myself in it many times trying to find my way back." He paused, hoping not to have to explain what Lilac would never want to hear. But Lilac did not budge, waiting for the rest of his story. Maurice looked to the side, sighed loudly, and continued. "The old lady from the cottage disappeared and I was left to care for her granddaughter. Things happened between us," he said as he looked in Lilac's eyes with pity.

Lilac's breath quivered with grief. She placed her hand over her chest as she felt her heart sink. Maurice continued, "We have two sons, Lilac."

Lilac's legs became weak. Her body slipped out of Maurice's grip as she gently fell to her knees, sobbing.

Johndor had been pacing back and forth and peeking out the window to check on Lilac. When he saw Lilac crying into her hands and Maurice just staring down at her without offering any solace, Johndor stepped outside.

"It's been a long day. The queen needs to rest now," Johndor said as he pulled her up from her knees, not taking his eyes off Maurice.

Maurice bowed his head at Johndor, respecting his advice.

"Johndor, if I may, I would like to take her up," he said. Maurice dried her tears and gently ushered her inside, holding her waist lovingly. She pushed her face into his shoulder, looking for his consolation as they made their way upstairs. He held her head on his chest and patted her hair, whispering in her ear, "Shhh, darling." The term of endearment broke her down further. Her sobbing was heard throughout the castle.

Maurice entered his old quarters with Lilac and closed the door behind them. He looked around the room. Nothing had changed. His eyes glossy, he took a deep breath as tears began to fall for the life he'd lost. His tears drove Lilac into his arms, where she cried uncontrollably against his chest. He guided her onto the bed and lay down next to her, still holding her head on his chest.

"Stay," she whispered, looking up at her husband. "We need you. I need you. I never stopped waiting, hoping, and praying. And now you're here."

Maurice kissed her on the lips and proceeded to undress her.

Chapter 23

Bethlynn tiptoed out of her room so as not to wake Isabella, and headed down to the kitchen. She wrapped her skinny white arms around Johndor in an unusually long hug and thanked him for preparing the tea. She soon returned to Isabella with the morning tea and scones Johndor had waiting for her in the kitchen and found the princess starting to wake. She set the tray on a table and sat next to Isabella on the edge of the bed. Isabella reached up and hugged Bethlynn, happy she had spent the night and shared some comical stories to comfort her until she could fall asleep.

"You're beautiful, Bethlynn. I wish I had your fine little nose."

Bethlynn smiled. "You are more beautiful, and young, and you may borrow my nose for a small price."

"Bethlynn, is father still here?" Isabella asked.

"Get yourself ready and we will go find out. I will take your mother her tea and be back for you."

Bethlynn knocked on Isabella's bedroom, where the queen had agreed to spend the night, to serve her with tea. Bethlynn then opened the door. Lilac was not there and the bed had been untouched. After being paralyzed in surprise for a moment, Bethlynn scurried back out to the hall to catch Lauren before she knocked on the queen's bedroom door with tea for the king. She tiptoed to Lilac's quarters and, ear to the door, she heard the king and queen's voices. With a gasp, she ran back downstairs on her tiptoes, careful not to spill the tea on the tray.

Lauren was at the bottom of the stairs. She appeared distressed and Rolf was embracing her in his arms. Bethlynn wished not to interrupt, so she passed them by, giving her sister a look of concern.

"Bethlynn!" Lauren cried out.

Bethlynn stopped and turned to her sister. "What is it, Lauren?"

Lauren looked at Rolf, fidgeting with the ruffles adorning the midline of his shirt. "Tell her, Rolf."

Bethlynn looked to Rolf to explain what could possibly have happened now. She had just seen Johndor, Isabella, Lauren and Rolf, and had heard the voices of Lilac and Maurice.

Rolf said, "We have lost Dr. Tottle." Bethlynn gasped, speechless, and looked back and forth at Lauren and Rolf.

Lauren sobbed. "I must find a midwife right away. How could this happen? First Minna, then Dr. Tottle. Who is next? They say death comes in threes."

"Now, now, Lauren," Bethlynn said. "You're beginning to sound like Lilac."

Johndor, who had been speaking with the priest in the sitting room, overheard Lauren and called for Bethlynn to come to the study.

Bethlynn patted her sister's shoulder and rushed to the study. "Yes, Papa?" she said from the open door of the study.

"Bethlynn, please ask Isabella to fetch some linden leaves for Lauren. Her nerves have gotten the best of her wits." He whispered to himself, "As they usually do."

Bethlynn nodded and turned to go back upstairs just as Isabella reached Lauren and Rolf at the bottom of the stairs. Isabella said, "I heard

Johndor. I'll be right back with the leaves. I will need hot water for the tea, please, Bethlynn."

"Hot water it is, Doctor," Bethlynn replied with a mischievous smile.

Johndor led the priest, his daughters, and his son-in-law to the chapel for an early mass. Noticing Lilac and Maurice were not there, he looked at Bethlynn. She took a deep breath and made her way upstairs very slowly, practically stomping to give warning that she was on her way to their room.

Reaching the top step, Bethlynn could hear their voices escalating. It didn't matter how hard Bethlynn stomped her skinny white legs, they were too enthralled in an argument, just like old times. She carefully placed her ear over the tiny space between the two doors and heard Lilac yelling as she usually did when she wasn't getting her way.

"You are my husband! And the father of Princess Isabella!"

Maurice shouted back, "Lilac, it was not my intention, but I cannot now leave my children, for they are not well."

"Your daughter... Isabella, is not well either, Maurice!"

"Lilac, please, the two boys are ill. Death could claim them at any time."

Lilac raged on, jealous and refusing to give Maurice up to another woman now that she had him in her grasp; no less a woman who had stolen him from her.

Maurice's anger at Lilac was growing by the second, and for a moment, he felt glad not to be her husband any longer.

"I will leave immediately after the burial!" Maurice yelled as he burst out the door, almost knocking Bethlynn to the ground. He grabbed Bethlynn to steady her. "My apologies, Bethlynn."

Bethlynn held her chest, gasping, then yelled into Lilac's quarters as she watched the king storm down the hallway. "We await your presence in the chapel to begin mass, ma'am!" She rushed through the hall and down the stairs.

At the bottom of the stairs, Maurice was grabbing Isabella's nose between his second and third knuckles, just as he used to when she was a tot. Isabella laughed respectfully and stared at him, waiting for a fatherly connection in the familiar exchange. She was saddened that he felt more like a stranger than a relative to her.

Chapter 24

Johndor pulled open the sapphire blue coach curtains. The smell in the air was familiar. They had reached Cuvington.

He shouted at Samuel, "Keep to the right!"

Thecemetery lay between the ocean and the east border of Cuvington. Isabella moved closer to Johndor to look out at the town she had heard so much about. Thebreeze blew her long blonde hair into her face. Bethlynn pulled Isabella's somewhat tangled hair into a bun as the princess stared out the carriage window, smiling because she was out and about, even if for a sad occasion.

Finally, seeing hundreds of tombstones scattered about on the right, Samuel stopped the carriage. Johndor let himself out and walked in between the tombstones, looking for his mother's. The structures he'd once used as markers had vanished, but he searched each one until he found it. Falling to his knees, he kissed the tombstone, then leaned his head forward in prayer. He stood up, examined the space around it, and waved, confirming he had found the perfect spot.

Samuel secured the carriage horses, went to the wagon carrying Minna's coffin, and grabbed the shovels. Rolf, Maurice, Father Marbone, and Samuel each took one corner of the wooden coffin, preparing to lead their procession. Bethlynn and Isabella spread Minna's favorite green and gold paisley tapestry over it. Lauren and Lilac whimpered as they watched. The ladies held hands and walked behind the men.

Father Marbone stood at the head of the cedar coffin and led prayers as Samuel and Rolf dug.

Each then took their turn stooping over the coffin, whispering their farewells, and rising back up in tears. Isabella set gardenia flowers they had picked along the way over the tapestry and kissed the coffin five times. Tears streaked down her cheeks as she laid her face on the coffin and trembled in sadness.

"Farewell, my Queeny. You will always be my Queeny. I love you with all my heart."

Johndor smiled. The rest shed tears watching Isabella. Johndor stood firmly, hands clasped in front of him, gaze unbroken, until everyone else had paid their respects and begun walking back toward the carriage. He bent down on one knee, whispered a couple of words, and gently tapped the coffin three times as if making sure Minna had heard his words.

On their way out of the cemetery, Lilac's steps quickly gained speed as she attempted to avoid Maurice.

In jest, to lighten up the mood, Bethlynn touched Lauren's round belly and laughed. "Ugly child, like his mother."

"Bethlynn!" Lauren struck Bethlynn playfully across her arm. Isabella pulled her hand over her mouth and laughed. Lauren pulled on Isabella's bun, loosening her long golden strands, and they all let out a chuckle.

Maurice reached for Isabella's hand, chuckling. "Not much has changed, I see."

Lilac replied, raising her voice for all to hear. "A lot has changed, I'd say!"

Maurice looked at Isabella. "And she hasn't changed at all."

Isabella laughed, nodding with confirmation.

Chapter 25

Two years had passed since Minna lost her life to the rare and unfortunate disease. Isabella had become more and more rebellious, fighting through her grief and desperation for independence from her mother and the confines of her castle prison, venturing outside of the castle against Lilac's orders. Minna had always given Isabella the motherly love Lilac just couldn't, and her last bit of joy had died with Minna.

Lilac became more and more bitter, only finding joy in a platonic relationship with Father Marbone that she had made up in her head. The father visited her regularly to ensure her healthy mental state after the shock of finding out Maurice had another family. Never did Father Marbone imply a feeling of romance, but Lilac was convinced otherwise. She was never the same after learning the truth about Maurice. She constantly imagined everyone was out to get her and Isabella.

She never once stopped to consider the impact Minna's death had taken on Isabella. Instead, she blamed the spell for her daughter's behavior and maladies. She often thought back on all the time and money she'd spent with Carmile and wondered if she had been deceived. Were Thumbeline and Johndor in fact right when they had warned her about Carmile's deceiving ways? Had her desperation clouded her judgement?

With no other options to help her daughter be the princess Lilac wanted her to be, she decided to give Carmile's advice one last chance. She remembered Carmile recounting how she'd reversed a spell on a child by changing the child's first name.

She could still hear Carmile say, "... and the curse became confused, and found its way out, in search of the girl whose spell it was about."

Lilac hadn't changed Isabella's name back then for fear of upsetting Maurice, as Isabella had been named after his mother. But now that Maurice's opinion was no longer of importance to her, and because Isabella's opinion had never been, Lilac began the legal process just days before Isabella's seventeenth birthday. According to Carmile, the number seventeen was of grave importance, and so, without informing Isabella, Lilac changed her name to Celeste.

Naturally, Isabella did not take the news lightly when Lilac presented her with a legal scroll with her name revised.

"You have finally gone bonkers!" she yelled. "You'd be bound to cut my leg off, wouldn't you, if you thought ridding me of my scar from the arrow would rid me of the curse?"

"Oh, Celeste... rubbish!"

That night, Isabella vowed to stay as far away from her mother as possible, fearing she might inflict more of her demented ideas on her. She spent many of her days behind closed doors in her chambers writing poetry to avoid her mother. Any necessary rapport between the two ladies was short and bitter.

By Isabella's twenty-second birthday, she still had not grown used to her new name. Only Lilac called her Celeste, and referred to her by her new name when speaking with the castle help. Yet, for the first time in many years, Isabella showed some sign of joy. She anxiously waited for Mr. Henderson, the butcher, on Tuesdays and Saturdays, hoping his son Chester would be riding with him. Chester was a tall, stocky, black-

146

haired boy about Isabella's age. He walked with a slight limp that was almost invisible to the eye.

Noticing Isabella's interest, Bethlynn whispered in her ear, "Boy's got a funny foot, ya know."

Isabella shrugged her shoulders. "That's alright with me. I'm far less than perfect."

Bethlynn shrugged, mocking Isabella. "Suit yourself then."

Isabella did, and after only one year, Chester and Isabella wed. She finally got her wish to live away from her mother when she joined the Henderson household in the Isle of Belfront. Whether she was infatuated, in love, or just in need of escape from her mother's ways, Isabella wasn't sure, and it didn't matter much to her. She treasured the freedom and desperately needed Chester's attention—sometimes too much, causing her to be jealous and clingy, which built a wedge of stress and unhappiness between her and Chester.

One evening, Isabella demanded that Chester not go to work with his father. After only a few months of marriage, she had grown too afraid that he'd meet another girl in the same way he'd met her. Chester's mother saw Isabella as a threat to the family business and convinced her son to legally divorce Isabella. Although he still loved her, Chester uttered words to Isabella that made their matrimony forever irreconcilable—he claimed she was just like her mother. Those words pierced Isabella's heart so deeply that she swore he would never hear from her again.

Isabella was forced to return to Fleurham and live with her mother. Lilac hated seeing her daughter as unlucky in love as she'd been. She decided to fix things once and for all after finding out that Isabella was spending her days in bed, crying into her pillow. She marched into the princess's room and tried to pull her out of bed by the hand, noticing she had switched her wedding ring to her middle finger because her fingers had thinned so much in the weeks since she'd come home.

"Celeste, you must come with me at once!" Lilac cried as she tried to get her daughter out of bed.

"I am going to die!" Isabella said, sobbing. "How can love hurt this much?!"

"Forget that now, Celeste. We must get your husband back, you hear me? Get up now!"

Samuel had already been instructed to bring the carriage and wait, despite it being dusk already. He set his concern aside and perked up when Isabella and Lilac appeared through the castle doors. He helped Isabella into the coach, noticing her thin arms. She had lost quite a bit of weight while refusing to eat or drink anything but scones and tea two times a day for the last month. He was tempted to voice his concern, but was afraid of Lilac's usual snide remarks.

"Where to, Your Majesty?" Samuel asked.

"Thumbeline's, please," Lilac said, then turned to check Isabella's reaction.

Willing to do anything to gain back her husband, Isabella slid over to make room for her mother. Samuel closed the coach door and started on their way.

For the next two hours, Lilac delicately ridiculed Isabella about how she had treated Chester. "You know, Celeste Isabella, you don't like to take orders. When you are married, you are to do as your husband says." Isabella rolled her eyes in disbelief that her mother would judge her at a time like this.

Lilac combed her fingers gently through Isabella's hair and softened her voice. "Luck hasn't been on your side for a long time now. You know this. You must play your cards right." Lilac nodded her head and clicked her tongue in pity. Isabella, too weak to argue, prayed to herself, *Please God, make her be quiet, please, please.*

148

Lilac continued, "I noticed how you often patronized him. As you do me."

Isabella responded in her head, *But you deserve it, you crazy cow.*

"And also Celeste," Lilac said, raising her tone, "you MUST eat! You look plain ugly!" Isabella took a deep breath and cocked her head to the side, away from Lilac, tricking her into thinking she had fallen asleep from fatigue for the rest of the trip.

Isabella recognized the passage and perked up in the seat. "Isn't this the path where the ugly old witch lived?" She shivered at the repulsive memory.

"Carmile. She's dead now, you know," Lilac replied.

Isabella was secretly grateful, having been afraid her mother might be trying to make her visit the old hag again.

Lilac pointed at Thumbeline's house. "That one over there is Thumbeline's house." Isabella saw the treehouse cottage in the distance and smiled at how amusing and unreal it seemed.

The two ladies approached Thumbeline's front door, which opened by itself. Lilac pushed Isabella in. "Quickly, quickly, step inside."

Thumbeline waited for Samuel to enter, then pushed the door shut with her walking stick. She laughed at Isabella and said, "You thought it was magic... the door that is." She waved her walking stick in the air. "It was!" She reached up for Isabella.

Isabella smiled and leaned down to hug the sweet old lady. She felt safe in her presence for some reason.

Thumbeline pointed at her pipe and bowl sitting on a small table. Samuel handed it to her. Thumbeline grabbed it, kissed his hands and grabbed the pipe with her lips.

"Shall we?" she said, gesturing to be pushed to her reading room.

"Go, Isabella." Lilac pointed to the back of Thumbeline's chair. Isabella, looking puzzled, walked behind Thumbeline.

"I'm sorry, I didn't know I was supposed to push." Isabella said sheepishly.

Thumbeline said around her pipe, "To survive in this world, you have to wake up, Isabella."

"Celeste," Lilac asserted. "Her name is Celeste."

"Ha! Didn't realize she had a twin!" Thumbeline smirked.

"By changing her name, the spell was confused and drawn away. That is why all this with her husband has happened to her, because she refused to be called Celeste," Lilac spat angrily.

Thumbeline took a drag from the pipe and blew out a twirl of smoke from her nose, then broke out laughing again. "The things we believe. The things we believe, Isabella— that is the real curse!" She pushed open the door of the reading room with her walking stick and pointed for Isabella to take a seat at the long table.

Lilac turned to Samuel just before entering the reading room. "Not a word of this, Samuel," she said very sternly, as she shut the door.

Samuel held his hands up as if surrendering. "Not a word."

Thumbeline looked Isabella up and down, observing her gaunt appearance. "You are too thin for your own good. Men like meat on a woman's bones." She rubbed her hands slowly up and down her thighs, taking deep drags from her pipe and blowing smoke out her nose like a dragon. "Why don't you like your mother, dear?"

Isabella replied candidly, ignoring her mother sitting next to her, "Because she is not well in the mind. She wants me to think like her. I don't want to be her."

"Therein lies the problem," Thumbeline said very slowly.

Lilac sat forward and blurted, "The problem lies in that she and Chester must reconcile at once. That damned cursed spell has ruined her life!"

Thumbeline nodded in agreement. "Ah, the cursed spell again. There is one God bigger than any curse," she said, staring at the glass ball sitting

150

to her right, surrounded with candles. "Some things are just not meant to be."

"Not meant to be?" Lilac said. "It must be, it must be. Please do something. She suffers... see how thin and ugly she has become."

Isabella looked down in shame. "Please, Thumbeline, I want my husband back."

Seeing the sadness in Isabella's eyes, Thumbeline reached in the drawer of the wooden desk and pulled out a small stone. She blew some smoke from her pipe and reached her hand out to Isabella's forehead. She tapped her forehead three times with the stone, murmuring some words in a strange dialect, then looked in Isabella's eyes and said, "Take this stone... and never lose it."

Isabella accepted it and held it tight in her fist, admiring the talisman that would make her husband return. She smiled.

Thumbeline watched the change in her face.

"This will bring him back, right?" Isabella said.

Knowing it was simply a good luck talisman, Thumbeline replied with only a smile.

Weeks passed, and although Isabella was in better spirits, her marriage remained divided and she still suffered secretly. She visited Thumbeline weekly, and they engaged in deep prayer and conversed on cosmic subjects. Slowly, Isabella outgrew her interest in Chester, despite Lilac's wishes.

Chapter 26

Months passed, and Isabella grew lonely. The cold winter was finally coming to an end, and the weather was better suited for traveling long distances. She requested Samuel take her to visit Thumbeline. She felt the need for her wise advice and her sweet comfort. She packed special herbs for her pipe as a gift.

Thumbeline was ecstatic to hear the young princess calling out her name from the front garden and wondered if she was bringing a new love story today so that she could relive her youthful days. The sensation lasted days for Thumbeline, who sometimes dreamed of love affairs in her sleep. She also looked forward to Isabella mocking and mimicking Lilac and any gossip from the castle, which Isabella transparently exaggerated, making Thumbeline laugh for hours. The two ladies drank tea and prayed and laughed. Thumbeline dismissed Isabella every time with a love story about her youth. Thumbeline's face lit up as she recounted her love affairs, especially the one with the tall professor from whom she continuously asked for private French lessons. "And the only words I can remember were 'Au revoir', as soon as I learned he was married. Means good-bye," Thumbeline said, chuckling.

Thumbeline warned Isabella just before this visit was over. "There will be a man in your life. Good hearted, spiritually sound. You must not fall in love, for happiness will not be found."

Isabella left Thumbeline's that day walking on air at the thought of a new love.

"Don't fall in love!" Thumbeline shouted as Isabella ran to the coach. Isabella waved farewell, paying no mind to Thumbeline's words.

Thumbeline was a hopeless romantic, even if it was someone else's love story. Isabella knew that and so she returned to visit Thumbeline just weeks later—despite Lilac's orders to give Samuel a break—to inform her about a new beau. For months Isabella had kept Samuel busy taking her all around town in search of different herbs. Perhaps in my search for exotic herbs, I will find an exotic beau, Isabella thought to herself.

Thumbeline picked dried leaves from different canisters, smelling each one and mumbling some words in a different dialect before dropping them into a jar half filled with water.

"Love potion," Thumbeline said excitedly.

Isabella's eyes opened wide. "Have I got to drink that?"

Thumbeline laughed, cocking her head back, then brought the pipe back to her mouth and took small drags. "Perfume, my dear," she said, as she held the jar to Isabella's nose. "Take a whiff."

Isabella carefully inhaled slowly. "Flowery, cinnamon..."

Thumbeline gazed into the clear goblet of water sitting on the table. "Show me this man the princess speaks of." She squinted and drew her head closer to the goblet. "A harmonious tongue has he."

"His name is Josiah. A musician he is. Plays the chordophone and sings like an angel," Isabella said excitedly.

Thumbeline inhaled deeply, annoyed at how Isabella, like her mother, always interrupted her trance. She stared intently at the glass and continued.

"A harmonious tongue has he... no good for you will he be."

She threw the water from the glass into a brass bowl, and proceeded to pray into the bowl. After several minutes, she turned to Isabella with an austere look. "Isabella, I must implore. There will be someone better for you. Do not delve any further into this romance."

Isabella had never seen Thumbeline communicate in such a serious manner. She asked no questions. Immediately, she broke all future engagements with no explanation, leaving her olive-skinned beau broken-hearted and forever wondering.

Two years later, Isabella learned that her gentle musician had died in a terrible freak accident while riding his horse. She wept in the arms of her new suitor, Danthony, filled with deep regret that the musician had died with a broken heart—a heart she had broken.

Danthony was a mature older man full of wisdom, yet he had the heart of a child. He admired Isabella's childlike, playful character. She admired the fatherly security and comfort he provided her. She had seen him a few times at Sunday service when she was married to Chester and had recently run into him during a run for a special herb that grew near the ocean at the isle.

Thumbeline loved the idea of Danthony all too much. She felt he could take her to the next level of womanhood. She would ask Isabella to tell her all about him and how he showered her with gifts, and often stared at the beautiful gold and onyx ring Danthony had gifted Isabella. She wore it on her right ring finger and the gold posy ring Chester had gifted her on her left ring finger. Thumbeline would sigh at the obvious charisma Danthony was blessed with. Sometimes Isabella thought Thumbeline herself was infatuated with Danthony—a thought that made Isabella chuckle when it came to mind, but which didn't keep Isabella from seeking Thumbeline's advice on how to keep her suitor.

Thumbeline looked into her goblet of water. Isabella's foot shook in suspense as Thumbeline took longer than usual to utter any words.

Isabella stared at the goblet, trying to see what Thumbeline saw, but all she saw was the copper bowl sitting behind the goblet. Thumbeline took a long, slow drag from her pipe and continued to stare, rubbing her thighs back and forth to deepen her trance.

"Mmm... mmm... mmm," Thumbeline said as she blew the smoke out the corner of her mouth, taking her time, dithering over whether to let Isabella in on all the details.

Isabella's heart beat faster.

"Very, very good potential," Thumbeline declared.

Isabella sighed, smiled widely, and relaxed the nervous tension that had built up while waiting for Thumbeline to say something about her reading. She dried her sweaty palms on the skirt of her dress.

Indeed, the potential was good, as Thumbeline predicted. The challenge would be in Isabella's patience at weathering future difficulties. Thumbeline only wished to still be around to guide her when that time came. "Isabella, you will have to grow up quickly with this one." Isabella perked up, with a questionable look on her face, and felt a smidgen offended.

"What exactly do you mean, Thumbeline?" Isabella asked in a slow, mature voice.

Thumbeline answered very matter-of-factly, "You must behave like a woman... a grown woman. If you do, you will have the world at your feet." Isabella's face flushed red with excitement as she clasped Thumbeline's hands in hers, knocking her pipe to the floor.

"So sorry," she said as she quickly bent down to pick it up.

Thumbeline replied, "No need, you will be able to buy me plenty." The two ladies laughed. Isabella hugged Thumbeline hard, and ran back to the coach, requesting Samuel take her to see Danthony right away. "Take me to the isle right away please," she demanded, with a big smile on her face.

156

Just as Thumbeline predicted, Isabella wed Danthony one year later in Belfront Abbey, the main cathedral in the Isle of Belfront, where Isabella had previously lived with Chester. For the first time, Isabella felt she was on top of the world. As she walked down the aisle, she searched for Lilac, hoping to finally receive a smile of approval, knowing Lilac hadn't favored the older man from the start. As she noticed Lilac turning around, Isabella quickly turned away to avoid anything ruining her big day. Danthony's many wedding guests were merry, singing loudly and joyfully all night long. Danthony joined them, singing songs Isabella was too young to know. She just laughed at the silliness.

Slowly but surely, difficulty began to rear its ugly head. The charming Danthony was very much admired by many women. Isabella's romantic experience had been limited, as she had not yet reached 30 years and had led a very isolated life under Lilac's control. Danthony, on the other hand, had had his share of experiences, and those past relations continued to interfere, with previous love interests continually pursuing him with no regard for the young wife.

Isabella, jealous, immature, and stubborn, ran to Thumbeline as she had done before in times of crisis. She threw herself on Thumbeline's lap, crying. "I will never find happiness... because of this curse... isn't that right?"

With concern at how distraught Isabella appeared, Thumbeline tapped the table repeatedly. "Sit down, sit down, little girl. Let's have a look at this curse that is to blame for all the wrongdoings of this world."

Thumbeline moved the goblet of water closer to her and rubbed it, muttering low in her mystical dialect, "Show me now... make it seen. Is there a spell... cursing the daughter of the queen?"

Thumbeline opened her eyes wide and the corners of her lips perked up in delight. Deeply entrenched in what was being shown to her, she failed to hear the knocking at the front door.

Isabella was afraid to interrupt, but the knocks became louder and longer. The banging soon made her jump to her feet. Thumbeline pointed to the front door while staying in her trance, gesturing for Isabella to see to it. Isabella gently closed the reading room door, then sprinted to the front door on her tiptoes.

Thumbeline's smile grew bigger and she clasped her hands together in prayer.

Isabella opened the front door to find a very tall, thin man dressed in dirty, ragged clothes, holding a long knife.

The man looked down at Isabella, his dark, beady eyes and expression making her wonder if he had a sick mind. "I seek Thumbeline," he said harshly.

Isabella's voice trembled with fear. "I will go get her straight away."

As she turned to run to Thumbeline, the tall man grabbed her arm and pulled her back. Turning her to face him again, he placed the knife to her navel. "Give me all your shillings!" he said savagely.

Shaking, she reached into her cleavage, where she kept a small purple velvet satchel filled with coins for Thumbeline. She loosened the cord of the pouch as the man tore it from her hands and emptied it into his. Isabella looked desperately for Henry, the coachman from her and Danthony's manor, praying he would arrive.

Thumbeline yelled with a concerned voice from her reading room. "Isabella? Isabella?"

The man grabbed Isabella's arm again, shaking it. He put his face close to hers and whispered, "Not a word to Thumbeline, or I will kill you."

The reading room door opened. Thumbeline tried to make her way out quickly as she saw the man shaking Isabella's arm. She yelled, "Oliver!"

Oliver dropped the knife and ran out the door.

Thumbeline shook her head in disappointment. "I am terribly sorry for him, Isabella. He is harmless and deadly terrified of me. Please hand me that knife... I can use it in my kitchen," she said, pointing at the knife by Isabella's feet.

At that precise moment, Isabella saw Henry approaching down the path in the distance. She ran out, slamming the door behind her. Oliver was still walking away and looked back at her. Isabella froze, then turned back and ran to Thumbeline's house. She rushed inside and held the door shut with her body, her chest heaving as she cried uncontrollably.

"Isabella, it's alright, dear. He is gone now."

Isabella heard Henry calling for her repeatedly. He had seen her run before he spotted the stranger. Isabella ran out the door and jumped into her coach.

"Go! ... as fast as you can... go! And do not stop for anyone or anything!"

She closed the curtains and threw herself to the floor of the coach to hide. She climbed to her knees slowly and opened the curtain slightly with her trembling hands to peek out and to make sure they had passed Oliver.

Thumbeline, quite upset at what had just taken place, opened the front door, shouting, "Oliver, come here at once! I dare you to do that again. I will personally slice your genitals off with your own knife and feed them to you!"

She waited, but Oliver didn't return. She pushed herself back inside and swung the door closed. "Coward!" she yelled as the door slammed.

Chapter 27

Many sleepless nights came to pass and Isabella suffered nightmare after nightmare of Oliver chasing her up a hill. She would wake with a jolt, trying to catch her breath and feeling like her heart would beat out of her chest. Falling asleep again was always a failed attempt.

For three months, Lilac tried relentlessly to convince Isabella to return to Thumbeline's. "She said she has a very good message for you, Celeste Isabella. She will not divulge it to me. You must not do this to Thumbeline, staying away like this. She feels terrible about what happened."

But Isabella trembled in fear at the thought of returning to Thumbeline.

Saddened not to see Isabella for so long, Thumbeline gave up summoning her about a year after the unfortunate incident.

Isabella endured the hardships of her marriage on her own for the next two years, until desperation forced her to seek advice from her mother when Danthony developed a drinking habit after a great loss of fortune due to a bad business decision.

Lilac, in her usual condescending manner, lectured Isabella. "I told you not to involve yourself with that man. But you are disobedient,

Celeste... as you have always been." Isabella sighed loudly. She had traveled an hour from the Isle of Belfront in the cold in search of her mother's guidance, only to be scolded.

Lilac's voice softened a bit to break the bad news to Isabella. "Celeste Isabella, Thumbeline has been very ill and her heart is very weak. You must go see her. I insist!" Lilac said softly, yet sternly. "We will all go together if we must. Bethlynn, Lauren, Samuel, and Johndor. I assure you I will kill that man with my bare hands if he tries something like that again. I am certainly not afraid of him, or anyone, for that matter."

Isabella gulped back her tears and agreed with a tentative nod of her head. "Please promise me we will stay no longer than half an hour," she begged, hands clasped together. "Please, Lilac."

Lilac nodded her head, still in disbelief that Isabella had never called her "mother" again after she changed Isabella's name to Celeste. "You have my word, Celeste Isabella," Lilac said with a concerned look, not having realized how deeply the near assault had affected her daughter. "I will inform Henry he may go back to the Isle. I will have Samuel return you home after the visit."

Isabella went to sit with Johndor in the study and tell him how Lilac had convinced her to go see Thumbeline. He'd fractured his ankle weeks earlier while he was helping Samuel untie the horses from the coach during a windy rainstorm and was managing the household from a chair until he could get around better. He instructed her to find hawthorn and white willow bark to make tea for Thumbeline. She knew exactly where it grew.

Isabella returned with a bushel of the two herbs, holding them up for Johndor's approval as soon as she entered the study door. Johndor smiled proudly as she brought them to him, then he wrapped the leaves in a white cloth and tied an old red ribbon around the bundle.

"Fabulous. Let's get a move on," Johndor said.

162

Isabella called for Samuel. He wrapped Johndor's arms around his shoulder. She grabbed Johndor's other arm and assisted him carefully to the coach as he limped, putting his weight on only the toes of his injured foot.

Isabella smiled, reminiscing about old times with Johndor and Bethlynn by her side. Feeling guilty, she blamed her troubles with Danthony for not visiting them more often. She leaned her head on Johndor's shoulder. He traced her face with his rough fingertips. The touch was so familiar and calming that she fell asleep for the whole trip to Thumbeline's. Lilac, Bethlynn and Lauren nervously spoke of what condition they might find Thumbeline in and grieved over how much time she might have left. The three reminisced sadly throughout the trip. Johndor remained quiet, concerned about Isabella.

Today, the door didn't open by itself. A maidservant opened the door and greeted them, inviting them in and showing them to Thumbeline's bedside. Samuel and Bethlynn assisted Johndor to the chair by Thumbeline's bed. Lilac held Isabella's hand and Isabella held Lauren's for emotional support at seeing Thumbeline lying impotent in her bed. Their eyes teared at seeing a skinny old woman who did not resemble the vibrant Thumbeline they knew. Her face was drawn and pale, her eyes sunken and dull. Her fuzzy gold hair was tied up in a bun at the very crown of her head. Sadness in her eyes also betrayed a trace of fear.

Thumbeline smiled as Isabella came into her view. Bethlynn and Lauren helped her sit up carefully and propped pillows behind her back. She stared at Isabella, who was standing quietly, nervous about Thumbeline's health.

Concerned that Isabella was uncomfortable, Thumbeline reached for Lauren and whispered weakly, "Go now, take her home."

Lauren nodded and ushered everyone out, but Isabella did not move. Thumbeline looked at Isabella, and Isabella at Thumbeline, as they engaged in a very deep connection. And although not a word was spoken, a profound love and forgiveness was exchanged. They both knew that would be the last time they would see each other.

Isabella hung her head low and walked out sadly.

Three days later, Isabella awoke with a heartbreaking feeling she could not explain. At the same time, Thumbeline's heart beat for the very last time, her message for Isabella... untold.

Chapter 28

An unkempt and anxious Isabella arrived at the castle, frantically looking for emotional ease from her unexplained heartache, to find that the coach was not there and only Johndor was available. He held Isabella's shaking hands as he sat her down at the kitchen table. "Isabella darling, Thumbeline passed in the middle of the night. Your mother, Bethlynn, and Lauren have gone to tend to her services."

Isabella whined like a little girl, "Why didn't they wait...?"

Johndor interrupted, "I stayed back waiting for you." Noticing Isabella's thinning frame, he took advantage and said, "You must first have a meal, then we will have Henry take us."

Johndor served Isabella a large helping of shepherd's pie, which she ate apprehensively and quickly, later burping it throughout the trip to Cuvington.

Johndor recounted stories to Isabella about when she was a baby for the next two hours to ease her mind and heart. Isabella listened intently, admiring how Johndor remembered everything about her. It made her feel special.

As they arrived on the stone path to Thumbeline's house, they noticed a caravan of four coaches in procession. Henry followed behind.

Isabella's heart beat faster in sorrow and remorse, remembering her times with Thumbeline and the times she missed. As they arrived at the burial grounds, she whimpered uncontrollably. She knelt down over the coffin and asked for forgiveness for never having gone back.

A saddened Isabella returned that evening to a drunken Danthony. She accepted that there was no hope and that their nuptials had finally crumbled, as had his entire fortune due to bad business decisions. Feeling guilty for both losses, Isabella surrendered to the cursed spell, giving up all hope for any chance at happiness. She moved back to Fleurham, and facing the cruel reality that Johndor was not getting any younger, she dedicated her time to learning about herbs from him. They spent every afternoon studying and testing concoctions, often using Bethlynn as a guinea pig. Bethlynn, who did not always like the taste of the teas, soon made a suggestion to Isabella: "Why don't you try your own teas? Perhaps you can cure yourself of your nightmares." Isabella stared at Bethlynn and pondered. Quietly she walked to the shelf of glass canisters that held tea leaves, picked out a select few, and concocted a blend for herself. After one week of drinking the tea, the nightmares had stopped and Isabella felt exhilarated at her ability to heal herself.

Still grieving the death of Thumbeline, she dared to ask Johndor, "Why couldn't herbs save Thumbeline?"

"Because, Isabella, we took her the next best herbs for her condition."

Isabella looked at Johndor with a perplexed expression wondering if she had picked out the wrong herbs. "Why didn't we take her the right ones?"

"Because, my dear Isabella, we cannot access those herbs."

"Why not, my sweet Johndor?" she said in a childish manner.

"The forest they grow in is in North Cuvington. It is now property of the French, so we're prohibited from entering."

A persistent Isabella, who had been sitting next to Johndor, moved herself to sit facing him and continued to question him adamantly.

"Why? What would have happened? What if nobody had seen us? It's only a handful of twigs. We could have saved her life."

Johndor smirked. "Ah… with the French, anything terrible is possible."

"But, Johndor, that was a long, long time ago. Maybe it's alright to enter now."

"I would not chance it. We have learned to live without the herbs now."

Isabella held both of Johndor's hands and looked him straight in the eyes. "Except Thumbeline. She couldn't live without them," she said, with a hint of frustration in her voice. Johndor took a deep breath and clicked his tongue in annoyance.

"What is it, Johndor?" Isabella asked, scared he might be upset with her.

"If I thought it was safe, Minna would be here today."

Isabella thought for a moment, then said, "If we can just grab a few different ones, we can plant them here and grow them ourselves. Maybe they are growing wild outside of the property and we wouldn't even have to enter. Just a quick grab as we ride by."

Johndor stared at Isabella, contemplating her idea. It was not a terrible one. Just a dangerous one, so he disapproved. He stood, ending the conversation.

Isabella walked behind Johndor, persisting, as he placed more canisters up on the shelf.

"Well, can Samuel just take us by to make sure it is still prohibited?"

"Can't hurt, I guess. There isn't a law saying we can't ride by. It is not a short trip though."

Bethlynn, having just walked in to wash the empty teacups on the tray she was carrying, said sternly, "I'm coming too! Where are we going, by the way?" she added jokingly. Isabella laughed.

Johndor answered, "She wants to go to Mulberry Hills. I told her we could ride by it, but not enter by any means."

Thrilled, Bethlynn jumped up and proclaimed in great delight, "Oh, the lovely flowers at the enchanted Mulberry Hills. I wouldn't miss this for the world! It saved my life, you know," Bethlynn said, matter-of-factly.

"Tell me how," Isabella said excitedly as she grabbed Bethlynn's and Johndor's hands and walked them to the table, eager to hear about Mulberry Hills.

Bethlynn put her hand on her chest to emphasize the conversation was now about her. "I suffered from asthma since I was an infant. I would visit the fortress at least twice in a week. The rich bushes of mint trees emanated their aromatic essence throughout the woods." Bethlynn took a deep breath and closed her eyes. "I can still smell it now." She straightened up and opened her eyes. "Anyway, the asthma would subside almost immediately."

Johndor went on to recount how he had saved Lauren's life as well. "She suffered a fever so high, it almost took her life." He explained, telling them how a delirious Lauren reluctantly sipped the sour tea he had made her. Within minutes she released a stool black as an onyx, and was instantly cured."

Isabella stared at Johndor, mesmerized at the power these natural remedies offered. "We must go then, we must go! I will tell Samuel he must take us tomorrow."

Chapter 29

When streaks of light sneaking through the curtains woke Isabella, she jumped out of bed and ran downstairs to check on Johndor and Bethlynn. Bethlynn was filling a wicker basket with scones, clotted crème, butter, jam and a warm baguette to sandwich ham and cucumber slices into. Isabella's heart filled with joy that their trip had not just been a dream. She turned and ran back upstairs, shouting over her shoulder, "I'll be ready in a minute, Bethlynn!"

Lilac stepped out of her quarters, half asleep. "What is all the ruckus about, Isabe—Celeste, I mean."

Isabella bowed her head and said sarcastically, "Pardon me, Queen Lilac. I will be leaving on a day trip with Johndor and Bethlynn."

Lilac squinted her eyebrows and slowly waved her away, then returned to her quarters. Isabella waited for Lilac to close the doors, then muttered under her breath, "You should really brush your hair now and then."

Isabella dressed in her most comfortable dress, a green cotton one with golden lace, donned a white bonnet, and jumped in the coach with Bethlynn and Johndor.

There was a youthful excitement in both women's eyes and Isabella eagerly clapped her hands like a child as the coach took off.

"Have you got the basket?" Johndor asked Bethlynn as he did off the four water flasks from around his shoulders.

"Yes," she said, tapping the top of the basket where it sat on her lap. "Ham and cucumber sandwiches and blueberry scones."

Isabella's face lit up again and she flashed her two large, wide front teeth. Johndor, puzzled, looked at Isabella. "Have you got the basket?" he said.

She laughed. "Johndor, you just asked Bethlynn."

Bethlynn circled her index finger close to her head, implying Johndor was bonkers.

Johndor fidgeted his fingers on his lap as he looked around as if someone was missing. He paused for a moment, then perked up and began to tell stories from his younger years. He told Isabella's favorite one from when she was a little girl, where he was riding a horse through the dark forest at the young age of fifteen. He felt a heavy load land behind him on the horse, and when he turned around, he saw a ghost of a man whose two front teeth were so large, they protruded from his mouth and extended down to his chin. "The ghost said, 'look at me teeth!' I pulled the reigns so hard, the ghost must have fallen off because he was gone the next time I looked," Johndor said, animated as no one had ever seen him be.

Isabella had always wondered if the story was a true occurrence or one he'd made up because her two big teeth had provoked a fable.

Bethlynn bucked her front teeth over her bottom lip, reached her arms out like a mummy, and murmured, "Look at me teeth, look at me teeth."

Isabella yelped, and they all laughed. An out-of-character Johndor laughed the loudest and longest.

Three hours and a half into the trip, Johndor looked out the coach curtains, checking their whereabouts. He asked Samuel to stop, then got out and rode in front with him. So much had changed, he was afraid they would go off track. He was also nervous to tread on prohibited territory. He took a deep breath, smelled bergamot and a touch of mint in the air, and knew they must be close.

Bethlynn looked outside. Isabella stuck her head out, unintentionally blocking Bethlynn's view.

"Isabella!" Bethlynn said sternly. "Move your big head."

"What are you looking for, Bethlynn?"

"Up to the right!" Bethlynn said loudly enough for Johndor to hear.

Ahead about half a kilometer down and to the left, she saw the largest tree in the woods, flourishing with white blooms.

"That's my favorite tree ever," Bethlynn said in delight, holding her right hand to her heart. "I've always imagined I'd marry under that almond tree."

Isabella looked at her, tempted to ask what had happened to him, but she saw the sadness in Bethlynn's eyes as she became deeply pensive. Isabella felt a sorrow in her heart for Bethlynn.

Isabella touched Bethlynn's hand. "Bethlynn, don't worry. One day we will both get married to the right one under that tree."

"But he was the right one," Bethlynn said, looking at Isabella with tearing eyes.

Isabella grasped Bethlynn's hand and said, "Will you tell me the story one day, Bethlynn?"

Bethlynn's demeanor changed to a more serious one. "It's quite short... the story. He was French. It was his country or me." She took a deep breath and noticed Johndor turn his head a few inches to eavesdrop.

"I thought he would come back for me. I waited and waited. Year after year. When he finally sent for me, Minna and Johndor refused to let me go. The conditions were life-threatening... and then... well, then life just went on."

Isabella smiled softly. "What was his name?"

Bethlynn stared at the enormous almond tree. "Bernard... Bernard was his name."

Thecoach came to a full stop, breaking Bethlynn's daze. Isabella stuck her head out the window. "Are we getting out now?" she asked excitedly.

Mulberry Hills had been fenced off with large wooden logs. A sign nailed to the gate and chained by thick, large links read:

Propriété du Ministère Royal Français.

Les intrus seront soumis à une sanction appropriée.

Property of the French Royal Ministry.

Trespassers will be subject to appropriate sanction.

Johndor stepped down as Isabella flew out the door. He clicked his tongue as he looked around. "What a shame to keep this healing meadow out of our reach." He clicked his tongue again, shaking his head in disappointment.

He pointed to different bushes and trees he could see from where they stood, explaining to Isabella each of their benefits. "That there is ulmus rubra, or slippery elm. It will heal sores almost immediately. But one must only apply at night."

Isabella wrote in her journal as Johndor led her past the many trees and bushes they could see from outside the fence. She captured location of plants, bushes, and trees; drew sketches of the many different leaves; and took short notes like "sores, night only."

Samuel and Bethlynn walked as close as they could to the giant almond tree without trespassing. They stared the lusciously flowering tree up and down, admiring its beauty.

Bethlynn noticed a small patch of grass under the shade of a large cedar tree not confined by the fence and pointed, saying, "There. Shall we have our lunch up there, Samuel?"

Samuel agreed and headed to the coach to fetch the basket.

"Don't forget the blanket!" she shouted at Samuel.

The four sat down and enjoyed the ham and cucumber sandwiches and scones. They ate slowly, relishing every second of the scenery and floral aroma of the enchanted forest while discussing how the French had stolen such beautiful countryside.

Isabella, developing her own feelings about the matter, blurted out, "Damned French!"

The three shushed her quickly. She looked down sheepishly, tapping her mouth. "Sorry," she whispered, laughing nervously.

Johndor stood and stretched, rubbing his full belly and looking around one more time. "Well, we best head out before the authorities ride by."

Bethlynn flapped the pink blanket in the air to rid it of crumbs, then folded it away in the basket. She walked to the coach with her eyes fixated on the almond tree, as if having a silent conversation with a glorious graceful goddess in white. She stepped up to the coach and handed Isabella the basket, then turned around one last time and bowed her head at the tree.

Johndor sat in the back again, trusting Samuel would know his way back. He smiled at Isabella as she looked out the window, taking mental notes of the path back to the castle. He looked at Bethlynn, who was mesmerized by beauty and memory, and decided to break her trance.

"When will we eat?" he said.

Bethlynn darted her eyes at Johndor with a very concerned look. "We just did," she said in a rising, high-pitched voice.

"Did we?" He laughed, then looked at Isabella and continued laughing.

Isabella felt a cold chill run over her. Her heart beat faster as she stared at an unusual Johndor. Something was wrong.

Chapter 30

Over the weeks after the trip to Mulberry Hills, Johndor's memory continued to decline. He repeated stories from his youth over and over. The end of one story was the prelude to the beginning of the same story, with no pause in between. Isabella listened as if it was the first time she'd heard them and chuckled every time.

On the other side of town, the very curious Maurice arrived at Glastonshire in search of answers. He visited Dr. Tottle's home in hopes that Roland, the strange man with the walking stick and the ghastly eye, would appear. Maurice had many questions for him.

After seventeen years, Maurice felt like he was finally waking from the spells Nan Marguarite and Maggy Mae had bewitched him with. He rode his horse through the entire village of Glastonshire asking about Roland's whereabouts. No one seemed to know who this Roland character was.

Maurice dared to describe him to a couple of young lads throwing stones in the river. "He's awkward looking... a little scary actually. Tall, uses a walking stick. His eye is kind of..."

The two boys looked at each other curiously. "Oh, you mean Pirate Eye?"

Maurice straightened up and squinted his eyebrows. It made total sense. He did look like a pirate from the sea. "Yes... Pirate Eye. Where does he live?"

The two boys laughed and continue to throw stones in the water, hoping for a ripple.

"Everywhere," the shorter boy answered.

The other boy nodded his head in agreement. "Yes, he lives everywhere."

"Everywhere?" a puzzled Maurice asked.

The taller boy continued. "Everywhere and nowhere."

"Last time I seen him was by the woods over there," the shorter boy said, pointing east by the edge of the river.

Maurice threw a couple of coins at the boys and headed into the woods, staying close to the edge of the river. As he reached the woods, he noticed a path disguised by large pieces of distressed driftwood scattered across the dirt. He stood at the edge and called out, "Mr. Roland! May I have a word? It's Maurice from Nokbershire."

No one replied.

Maurice looked around but didn't dare enter for fear of becoming lost. He got off his horse and stood close to the driftwood path, calling out again. "Roland! Mr. Roland! Are you here?"

Suddenly he felt a tapping on his boot and looked down. The gold tip of Roland's walking stick was knocking on the side of his boot.

"Good day, sir," Roland said.

Maurice turned and looked up quickly, bewildered that he had not seen Roland appear. "What? Where did you come from?"

"Ayyy, that's not important," Roland said. "What can I help you with and what can you help me with? Now that is important."

Maurice quickly understood he would have to pay for any details Roland might divulge.

"What do you know about Nan Marguarite?"

Roland nodded his head. "Ah-ha. Took you some time, but I always knew you'd come back for more." He pointed his walking stick into the woods, gesturing for Maurice to walk deeper into the woods with him.

Maurice tread carefully, avoiding the driftwood planks as he followed Roland. After about ten feet of moving branches and bushes off of the path, they came to a halt at a large square of land covered with polished driftwood. Maurice saw a wooden chest to the left and a chair ornately engraved with gold paint made out of pieces of wood tied with old rope and an old, faded red cushion on top. A tree stump posed as a table holding a lantern and a goblet. Ledges of wood tied with rope from the trees held books, cups, and other curious objects. A fire burned in a stone ring next to the wooden chest. On the far end, a myriad of colorful blankets and rags and one round seat cushion were arranged as bedding.

Maurice was speechless, in awe of this outside home where Roland resided. He instantly understood that Roland was homeless and why he was fearless and demanded payment for nearly every word he let out of his mouth.

Roland pointed at the wooden chair with his stick. Maurice sat down respectfully. Roland placed the copper goblet and lantern on the ground and sat on the tree stump table facing Maurice.

"Marguarite... ha... the ol' witch. Not her fault really. Legend has it her mother took some concoction. She wasn't married, you see. The poison she drank didn't do the job, and she birthed a baby girl with silver hair. They called her Metalhead."

He took a gulp from the copper goblet and offered it to Maurice. Maurice refused with a swift hand gesture.

Roland continued. "You know what they say?"

"What do they say?" Maurice asked patiently, with a bit of sarcastic angst in his tone.

"They say history has a way of repeating itself. They say Marguarite grew and became a maidservant for the prestigious Inchaustegeaux family."

Maurice swallowed hard and became suddenly tense. He didn't take his gaze off Roland so as to not interrupt.

"The youngest son, Ernest, was quite an inamorato, if you will. Word has it he used his golden hair, blue eyes, strong jaw, and good looks to his advantage. Marguarite, smitten at how he even minimally acknowledged her, fell weak to his desires and let him bed her."

Roland leaned closer to Maurice and whispered, "They say he made her wear a headdress. You know... cover her hair up." His voice rose again. "Ey! As if she hadn't had enough already. Well, it gets worse. You know what they say about history, ay?"

Maurice just shook his foot, anxious for Roland to get on with the story.

"Well, as nature would have it, she became with child and was dismissed from the Inchaustegeaux Manor after Ernest denied all accusations of loving Metalhead. His parents forced him to marry Victoria, daughter of the Duke of Elyngton, who birthed one boy... Patríc."

Maurice took a deep breath to calm his quickly growing frustration.

"Well, a gullible Victoria could not handle Ernest's ways with women. Her father, the Duke of Elyngton, had her brought back home, leaving Ernest and the Inchaustegeaux family in shame. That Ernest... a real ladies' man, he was." Roland took another sip from the goblet and stared into nothing.

Maurice uncrossed his legs and leaned forward to get Roland's attention. "What happened to Marguarite? Did she birth a child or not?"

Roland cocked his head to the side, noticing desperation in Maurice's voice. "Did we speak shillings? I don't believe we did. Ha, we must have forgotten with all the pent-up excitement about the ol' witch."

Maurice reached into his vest and pulled out two coins, then dropped them in Roland's palm.

"Yeh, I'll take half now. Thank you, sir," Roland said as he shoved the coins into a small brown leather pouch he wore across his shoulder.

Maurice took a slow, deep breath and asked again, very slowly, "Did she have the child?"

Roland nodded his head. "Did she have the child? Did she have the child?"

Maurice mildly slapped the arm of the wooden chair, embittered at Roland's intentional stalling.

Roland straightened in his seat. "Tale goes like this. Metalhead was said to wait for Ernest outside the Inchaustegeaux grounds in the hopes of convincing him to acknowledge their unborn child as his. Ernest had her removed and transferred back to her home in Nokbershire by two king's men, with the threat that if she returned, she would be imprisoned indefinitely. They took her away kicking and screaming, threatening a curse on the Inchaustegeaux family that would cut off the blood line if her child was not recognized as royalty. 'You will never get rid of me!' she yelled over and over as the two king's men dragged her away."

Roland stood and poured more ale into his goblet. Maurice reached into his pocket and pulled out three more coins, but kept them in his closed fist. "Well?"

Roland gulped in anticipation, then continued. "Oh yes, yes... a girl. Marie. Looked nothing like the Inchaustegeauxs. Made everyone wonder if she was telling the truth. But then again, not many, if any at all, would have bed Metalhead, if you know what I mean."

Roland scratched his head. "I mean, I can only see outta one eye, and I still wouldn't."

Maurice tried not to chuckle. "Where is Marie now?"

Roland looked down as he stood up and paced slowly.

"They say Marie died of sadness while giving birth. Her mother, Marguarite tried to break this 'child out of wedlock' curse when the girl was about sixteen and became pregnant. She forced Marie to marry the father-to-be at first notice she was with child. Name was Morch. Short for something French I recall. A bit violent that one. Marie begged her mother to let her raise her child on her own, but Marguarite wouldn't have it. Being shamed once was bad enough. Being shamed twice... well, that sounds like the beginning of a curse. Sad, really."

Roland walked back to the stump and sat.

"Marie's beau Morch refused to marry her, forcing Marguarite to raise her granddaughter—Little Maggy Mae, they called her— Marguarite grew angrier, swearing to take revenge on the Inchaustegeaux descendants."

Maurice sat back in his chair, stiff from shock.

Roland stretched out his leg and tapped the bottom of the wooden chair to break Maurice's trance. "Alright in there?"

Maurice shook his head in disbelief. "Yes, yes... trying to grasp this outrageous drama."

Roland scooted to the edge of the stump to lean closer to Maurice and whispered, "You look like a good man. How'd you end up in that retched, bewitched house anyway?"

"Why do you say bewitched?" Maurice asked.

Roland straightened up, pulling one shoulder back and turning his head while still looking at Maurice. "Oh, c'mon... everyone knows if you need a potion-tea, it's Marguarite you need to see."

Maurice clenched his teeth in anger and his ears turned red at the memory of his first encounter with Marguarite. He could almost taste the tea as he recollected that dreaded day.

Roland continued. "Wonder what happened to her anyway. Rumor has it she just fell off the face of the earth. Do you know, Maurice?"

Maurice shrugged his shoulders. He struggled to remember much after taking shelter from the storm, until Maggy Mae was pregnant with his child.

"By the way, I never got your full name, Mr.... What shall I call you?" Roland said.

"Maurice is just fine."

"Well, now, your blue eyes, your blonde hair... strong jawbone. Uh, you wouldn't be an Inchaustegeaux, would you?"

Maurice flared his nostrils, stood up quickly, pulled five more coins out of his pocket to add to the three he had been holding, and slapped the coins into Roland's hand.

"Not a word of this, you hear!"

Roland pinched his lips with his fingertips as Maurice raced out and jumped on his horse.

The realization that he and Maggy Mae were cousins sent a cold chill up his spine and an angry heat filled his head.

Chapter 31

Maurice confronted Maggy Mae with all the information he had just found out. She denied every bit of it, angering Maurice further. His anger over being tricked finally gave him the courage to leave her. "I never want to see your face again!" he shouted to her as he slammed the door behind him.

Maggy Mae ran behind him, yelling and crying, "If you leave, you will never see your boys again!"

Maurice turned back and walked close to her. He said, angry and slow, "I assure you, if they survive to grow up, they too will leave their fraud of a mother and will find their way to me." He raised his hand as if he was about to slap her. Maggy Mae raised her arms up in defense. Maurice flared his nostrils and stared her deep in her eyes. Then he turned and left.

He moved back to Fleurham, to a small structure belonging to his father's uncle about five miles away from Isabella and Lilac. He participated once again in Isabella's life, visiting his boys in Nokbershire every now and then after having a path structured to ensure safe travel to the small village.

Lilac's anger had only grown towards Maurice over the years, yet they were amicable with each other and he was always welcome at the castle.

She busied herself taking on more responsibilities since Johndor couldn't manage any longer the treasury Queen Catriona had left him in charge of. Her depression deepened as she learned how depleted the treasury was. Johndor had always felt obligated to give Lilac what she requested—after all, she was the inheritor—and his secret guilt about giving her to the Snow Queen had always been there.

Johndor's health declined over the next three years until, bed-ridden, he recognized Isabella only at random times and he mistook Bethlynn for Minna every time he saw her. One rainy morning in June, Isabella woke Bethlynn screaming for help. She burst out of her room and dashed toward Johndor's room.

"Papa, wake up! Wake up, Papa! she cried.

Isabella ran in and jumped on Johndor's bed, straddling him to feel his heart for any sign of life. She brought her mouth to his right ear and whispered, "You come right back, Johndor, right now! It is not your time. Come back, Johndor. Come back!"

A very faint sound came out of Johndor's open mouth. "I... I... I'm here," he whispered feebly as he struggled to open his eyes.

Isabella looked into his dull eyes, finding a halo of blue around his brown pupils. She kissed his cheek, laid her head on his chest, and cried softly. "You scared me, Johndor," she whispered. He reached out his hand ever so slowly and patted her head gently.

Isabella perked up and jumped down off the bed. "I'm going to make you the best tea ever!" She gave a shaky Bethlynn a hug and ran out to the woods in search of the perfect leaves.

As she walked between the bushes and trees, she heard a flapping sound from the trees. Three sprigs of long leaves fell from above and landed at her feet as a white dove flew out from between the high branches. Isabella, trusting her intuition and respecting omens and signs, picked up the leaves and took them back with her. She would need Johndor to tell her what they were for, as she did not recognize them. She only hoped Johndor still could.

Isabella walked in on a complaining Johndor as Bethlynn propped him up with pillows.

"Put my shoes on immediately!" Johndor demanded.

Bethlynn held his shoulders and looked him in his angry eyes. "Johndor! You are not going anywhere. You do not need shoes!"

Johndor made an angry face at her, scrunching his eyebrows and nose to mimic Bethlynn. "I must go to my mother's house," he replied, as his weak voice attempted to escalate. "She needs the cucumbers in my bag!"

Bethlynn and Isabella looked at each other and laughed. Bethlynn proceeded to put Johndor's shoes on him, as she felt disobeying her father even in these conditions was disrespectful.

Isabella showed Johndor the leaves. "Look, Johndor. Look what I found."

He tried to pull himself up for a closer look, but wasn't strong enough. She held the sprigs closer to him.

"Let me see, dear," he said as he tried to reach for them. Isabella placed one sprig in the palm of his hand.

He examined it, then rubbed his thumb back and forth to feel the texture of the leaves. Finally, he smelled it and began to laugh. "Olea europaea," he said joyfully, referring to the olive tree branches. "How did you reach up there?"

Isabella shrugged her shoulders, feeling victorious. "They just fell to my feet as a white dove flapped away from inside the branches." She sat next to Johndor and rubbed the leaves to memorize what she'd just learned.

Bethlynn stood by the armoire folding linens and nodding her head at the lucidity that had quickly overtaken Johndor. At times, she accused him of pretending he was not well. She did not understand how his character transformed so much, so quickly, in the presence of Isabella. Lilac walked in frantically, having heard Bethlynn yelling earlier. She stood by the foot of the bed with a puzzled look.

"What are they for, Johndor? Do you remember?" Isabella asked, ever so curious.

An excited Johndor suddenly found the energy to prop himself up. "What is it good for, you ask? Absolutely everything," he said full of vigor. "It is the symbol of heavenly power. When in doubt, Olea europaea."

Isabella smiled and tried to pull the sprig from his hand to go get the tea started. He pulled the sprig up to his nose, taking Isabella's hand with him, and took two quick but strong whiffs, wetting the bottom of the sprig with a bit of dribble from his chin. Isabella leaned in to take a waft of the leaves.

"Celeste! You will get sick. The leaves are dirty from his dribble!"

A startled Isabella looked at Lilac, angry and insulted that she had referred to Johndor as dirty. She stood, took the sprig from Johndor's hands, and held it to her face, taking a long, deep breath while glaring at Lilac. "You see, Lilac, when you do things from love, you don't get sick." She kissed Johndor's face, looking at Lilac from the corner of her eye.

"Celeste! Not with your luck!" Lilac yelled, trembling in anger.

Isabella held her head up proudly and walked past Lilac. She asked Bethlynn to make Johndor's tea while she fetched more of the olive sprigs before nightfall. Given the height of the tree, she felt luck must have been on her side that day, or perhaps on Johndor's, and she wanted to take advantage while she could.

Bethlynn brewed the tea to Isabella's precise instructions, then handed Johndor the teacup.

"Who are you, little lady?" Johndor said to Bethlynn.

"I am your tea maker for the day. Now please drink it," Bethlynn replied.

186

Johndor laughed as if he had been told a funny story. "But I don't drink tea, Catriona."

Isabella walked in empty-handed. She sat on the bed next to Johndor and brought the teacup to his lips. "But you must try this one... it's magic."

He took a sip, smiled, and gleefully said, "Thank you, Isabella. Your teas are so delightful."

Bethlynn quickly brought her hands to her hips and shook her head in disbelief. Isabella laughed. Johndor looked at Bethlynn, then looked at Isabella and whispered, "Who is that lady standing there?"

Bethlynn turned and walked away, as Isabella made up a story about who Bethlynn was. "They call her Lady Petunia. She is a splendid poet. She comes to rhyme..." Johndor interrupted.

"I'm sorry, Isabella dear. Would you please put on my shoes?"

"Johndor, your shoes are on."

"Yes, yes. Well then, can you please take them off?"

Although the "magic tea" did not bring back Johndor's memory, it sustained him for a good year. Isabella knew Johndor would not be around forever, so she spent most of her time with him. She regretted not having spent more time with Minna. Every day, she could see that Johndor spoke less and slept more.

One afternoon while grooming him, she pulled out a stubborn hair growing in the curve of his nose. She was tempted to keep it in a locket, but instead pressed it between his thumb and hers.

"Make a wish, Johndor," she said sweetly.

He smiled, not conscious of what she was saying.

Isabella felt a deep pull in her heart at watching Johndor become more and more emaciated. She gave him a peck on his forehead.

"Good night, Johndor. I love you."

She headed back to her chambers feeling a sadness in her soul as she thought about the inevitable. She lay in bed staring out her window at the dark sky. She contemplated life and death until she fell asleep. She no longer suffered from nightmares, but from other strange instances where she felt she was stepping outside of her body. But this time was different. She heard the insisting voice of a woman.

"You must check on Johndor," the voice said. Startled, Isabella opened her eyes and sat up on her bed to find no one in her chambers.

She threw her covers off and ran downstairs, into Johndor's quarters. At first, she didn't recognize his face and took a step back. Then his face changed right in front of her, to another face she didn't recognize, as if different people were passing through him. He closed his fists, his body became rigid, and his eyes rolled back and his mouth opened slightly.

Isabella began to tremble and she yelled out for help. "Bethlynn! Bethlynn! Lilac! Please, someone!"

Isabella laid her face on his chest, wetting his garments with her tears, and whispered to his heart, "Don't go, Johndor... don't go."

Her heart beat faster and her legs shook uncontrollably. She tried to unclench his tight fists, but gave up and kissed his hands instead. She watched his abdomen rise as he took a deep breath, then unclenched his fists slowly.

Bethlynn rushed in to find Isabella sitting on the floor barefoot, leaning against the pink and gold paisley embroidered armchair next to Johndor's bed. She was holding one hand to her chest and the other was cupping her forehead, trying to slow her racing heart.

Bethlynn grew wide-eyed and her cheeks turned red. "Isabella, what's the matter?"

Isabella couldn't reply through her sobbing.

Bethlynn approached Johndor and touched his warm skin, sighing with relief.

Isabella tried to tell Bethlynn what had happened. "He... he... he died on me, Bethlynn. Then he came back. No... no... no one came when I called out. I was so scared."

Bethlynn sat on the chair and stroked Isabella's hair to calm her. "I came as fast as I could when you called. You know my old knees slow me down a bit these days."

Isabella hugged Bethlynn's legs and cried on her lap. "I was so scared."

Bethlynn teared up as she cocked her head back to take a deeper breath. "Isabella, do you know how old Johndor is?"

Isabella looked up at Bethlynn, waiting for the answer.

"He is ninety-five years old. Almost a century, the old geezer, but he is tired. Nobody wants him to die, but he will one day, Isabella, and probably sooner than later."

Isabella wiped her tears.

"You must be ready, Isabella. You must let him go when the time comes."

She laid her head back on Bethlynn's lap and stared at Johndor laying on the bed, barely breathing. Her tears trickled onto Bethlynn's powder-blue dress.

For the next few days, Lauren and Rolf visited with their newborn. Lauren sat close to Johndor's bed and held his hand, feeling badly she had not visited often, as she had been ordered bed rest to prevent a second mishap. Maurice joined them also. They sat around Johndor's room chatting and carrying on as if he was one of the guests, although he was hardly conscious.

Evening came earlier on the cool October days, so the guests departed before sundown, leaving Isabella alone with Johndor. She stared at Johndor staring into space, wondering what might be going through his mind.

She drew her face close to his, holding her long hair back, and whispered, "I love you so much."

Johndor breathed deeply as if he were taking in the essence of her words. "Me... too," he said slowly, struggling for strength.

She kissed him on his wrinkly forehead, dried his dribble with her handkerchief, and walked away quickly, trying to contain her emotions.

Isabella slept the next two nights on the floor next to Johndor, on a makeshift bed constructed of throw pillows and blankets over a thick tapestry on the cold floor. On the third night, Bethlynn begged Isabella to sleep in her own bed. Exhausted from the restless nights on a hard floor, Isabella agreed.

Bethlynn looked at Isabella's worried face. "Don't worry, Isabella. I will sleep in the chair tonight to keep watch. If I lie on the floor, you will need an armada to lift me up in the morning."

Isabella grinned slightly and kissed Johndor's warm head. She held his hand in hers, feeling his soft palms and swollen, bony knuckles. "Good night, Johndor," she said sweetly. "Good night, Bethlynn."

Bethlynn watched Isabella as she walked away. She waited for the door to close. "Stubborn girl," she said to Johndor. "Just like her mother," she said, continuing to prop up his legs with pillows when she noticed he was gasping for air. She dropped the pillow and tried to sit him up, but his limp body flopped to the side. She called out for Isabella, who had just walked out a minute before.

"In God's name, help me," she said, frenzied, as she laid him back down. She looked heavenward, holding her head with both hands, tears rolling down her flushed cheeks as she tried to regain her composure. Nervously, she called out for Isabella again.

As Bethlynn looked back down at Johndor, his body twitched. It twitched a second time and then a third, and his gasping subsided. She shook him gently by his shoulders, realizing his eyes were fixed open. His stare was blank, his breath extinguished, and his spirit... departed.

"I forgot my pillow," Isabella said as she walked back into the room.

Startled, Bethlynn held her breath and stared up at Isabella. Her face was as pale as a ghost's and her eyes drooped in sadness.

Isabella knew the inevitable had happened. She cupped her hands around her nose and mouth and ran to Johndor's side. She held his hands, still somewhat warm, yet lifeless.

"Bethlynn, are you sure?" Isabella said as she laid her head on his chest, searching for a heartbeat.

"Yes, Isabella. Yes."

Isabella placed her lips on his forehead as she whispered, "May the Lord keep you in his glory."

Tears dropped from her eyes into his, giving them back their shine. She closed her eyes and kissed his forehead ever so slowly, then closed his eyelids forever.

Johndor was laid to rest next to his beloved Minna in Cuvington.

Chapter 32

Five years passed after Johndor's death. Isabella turned Johndor's old sleeping quarters into a private study. She furnished the sleep chamber with a large rectangular wooden table she used as a desk on which to study and concoct herbal remedies, and she placed all the books she had collected on wooden shelves hung on the stone walls.

She displayed Johndor's gadgets throughout, using them as inspiration. She hung a pair of metal scissors from a nail over the desk. It was a tool that often went missing in the castle, as it was often borrowed by the staff, upsetting Johndor when it could not be located. She displayed his metal cup, using it as a container for her pens, and his reading spectacles hung over the gold cord wrapped around the green curtains. She decorated the study with all she could find that belonged to Johndor, except his arrows. Within his belongings, Isabella had come across various arrows he had collected throughout his life. She was intrigued by the arrows, and at the same time felt an inner resentment towards them. She felt it was an arrow that had been the cause of her and her family's demise. She would sit and look at them every so often, trying to recapture the dreaded day an arrow changed her life.

On this day, she was tempted to explore the arrows. She sat on the floor in front of the metal box and pulled out the first arrow, which lay on top of others. She ran her finger up and down the black metal, examining every inch of the weapon. She felt anger and excitement at the same time as she faced her enemy. The idea to display them crossed her mind. Instead she quickly but carefully placed them back in the chest as she heard Bethlynn walking down the hall calling to her.

"Isabella, I'll be out in the garden."

An excited Isabella grabbed the rolled-up diagram from the wooden table and ran out of the room, delighted to start building an herbal garden with Bethlynn's expertise. The two ladies intended to plant herbs, vines, bushes, and anything that sprouted healing ingredients. Isabella had drawn up the design of what the healing garden would look like. She chose the lot located just off the right side of the castle's exterior where, according to Bethlynn, the rich moist soil was perfect for successful growth. She claimed it was because the chapel windows graced the wall where the garden began.

Isabella joined Bethlynn in the garden. The sun had just risen and Bethlynn was bent down, examining the soil with one hand and holding three empty tin baskets in the other when Isabella tapped her on the head with the large roll of paper, startling her. "You cheeky little lady... you shouldn't scare old people like me."

Isabella chuckled and rolled open the large sheet, showing Bethlynn the design for the garden. Bethlynn chuckled, as all she saw were sticks scattered about the page. "Is this your arithmetic homework?" Bethlynn said jokingly. "Now let's go, Samuel is waiting."

Samuel took them one hour west along the coast to visit a wooded area neither of the ladies had ever been to. Isabella took that time to explain her diagram to Bethlynn. Bethlynn pressed her lips together, holding in her laugh, as she did not want to break Isabella's inspired demeanor.

Samuel stopped at the entrance to the forest. Isabella rolled up the diagram, grabbed the baskets, and let herself out of the coach as Samuel helped Bethlynn out. "Samuel, we will need your assist to pull some shrubs out of the ground," Bethlynn said as she wrapped her arm around Samuel for support and began walking on the uneven terrain into the woods.

After two hours of pulling shrubs, twigs, and leaves, they returned to the coach with baskets full. Isabella examined their gatherings, smelling them and nibbling some of the leaves. Bethlynn sighed and pulled Isabella's arm away from her mouth. "You don't want to poison yourself, now." Isabella laughed confidently, feeling invincible from her successful acquirement.

The three arrived back at the castle and made their way directly to the garden. Isabella pulled out her diagram and laid it on the ground. She placed four small stones on each corner to hold it down. Bethlynn looked up at the sky, "Oh my! This calls for some tea and scones... and ale." Samuel chuckled to himself as Bethlynn made her way to the kitchen, laughing to herself.

Isabella directed Samuel where he needed to dig according to her diagram. She followed behind, planting the shrubs with her bare hands and sliding the soil back into the hole. She then pointed her dirty finger to the next location. Samuel noticed Bethlynn setting up the tea tray and lowered the shovel. Isabella picked it up and continued to dig passionately, ignoring the tea and scones. Bethlynn and Samuel enjoyed their tea, watching Isabella defiantly dig the shovel down with two hands wrapped around the dirty wooden pole, letting out a grunt. They both quickly joined her when they saw Lilac take a peek through the chapel window. By the end of the daylight, they had cultivated an herbal garden.

"Johndor would be so proud," Isabella said as she stood before the garden admiring their work of art. She smiled widely, the corners of her mouth trying to reach her ears. Her two large front teeth showed in their entirety.

Bethlynn, sweaty and red-faced from the heat, took a look at Isabella.

"Do you know the story about the ghost that jumped on Johndor's horse?"

Isabella covered her mouth with her dirt-covered hand and chuckled.

She walked around the garden collecting twigs and leaves from the plants she had just planted and then separated them out into small pieces of white cloth. She handed them one by one to Bethlynn.

"This is for Lauren, for her nerves."

"This is for Rolf, for his digestion."

"This is for Samuel; he's got terrible sniffles."

Word got around that Isabella was mixing herbal remedies for townspeople, peasants, and royals alike. She traveled around from town to town in search of apothecarists willing to take in an apprentice. She was exhilarated, learning of the magic nature offered, but had no luck finding an apothecarist who could teach her more. She had finally found a deep internal happiness, but longed for more knowledge.

She had Samuel take her to the Isle of Belfront in search of an old woman her prior husband Danthony, had told her about years before. The old woman practiced healing magic and had cured many. Samuel and Isabella left Fleurham at sunrise and arrived just about an hour later. The smell of fresh baguettes filled the air. Samuel stopped in the town center and let Isabella off. She walked around and asked all the townspeople who looked courteous enough to be bothered. She stopped to ask a woman carrying a baby.

"I'm looking for the old lady apothecarist... they say she's magic,"

Isabella said excitedly. The woman, bouncing the infant up and down, suddenly stopped and looked at Isabella sadly.

"Oh dear! She died many years ago."

Isabella frowned in disappointment. The woman continued. "Perhaps 20... maybe 30 years ago."

Isabella perked up. "That's not the one then. This lady was still alive 10 years ago," she said and walked away quickly, in fear that the woman would give her some type of bad news. She continued to ask around, to no avail.

Samuel watched Isabella's excitement quickly dwindle. He figured it would be best to ask those who looked like they'd been around a while. He approached an old man doing cobbler work on a piece of wooden board outside a tall, narrow stone house.

The short, white-haired old man looked up and fixed his spectacles.

"New to the isle?" he asked.

"From Fleurham, sir."

"Fleurham," the old man chuckled. "Well, welcome," he said as he continued to shape a piece of black leather. Samuel interrupted him again.

"Looking for an apothecary lady... very old... some claim she heals with magic."

The old man looked up at Samuel. "What do you need healed, son?"

"Oh no, not..."

Isabella interrupted Samuel. "No luck... I give up," she said to him. Samuel stepped aside, allowing Isabella to come fully into the old man's view. The old man stared at Isabella as if he knew her.

"Come closer, dear," the old man said. He looked into Isabella's eyes. Slowly, he put down the black leather boot and the metal, spoon-shaped object he held. He pointed his curved index finger at her.

"Wait here," he said.

The old man walked in the stone house, very slowly, watching his every step. Isabella and Samuel looked at each other. Samuel shook his head as Isabella shrugged her shoulders, both perplexed.

After a few minutes, the old man walked back out, his head hung low and with a less spirited demeanor.

"My apologies, I can't help you."

He picked up the boot and continued to work on it, ignoring Isabella and Samuel, who were still standing before him, curious and confused.

Samuel looked at the stone house and noticed a small window upstairs. He stepped back to take a better look when the curtain behind the window quickly pulled closed.

They heard a loud thump from inside the house. The old man startled, dropped the boot, and walked back in. Murmuring came from inside. The old man opened the door and gestured for Isabella and Samuel to step inside. The frustrated man complained, "I tell her and tell her, but that Pippa, I tell you, she is a stubborn one... very stubborn." He gently pushed Isabella toward the old, squeaky, wooden staircase. "Up there dear, she's up there," he said, then guided Samuel to sit in the front room as he made his way to the front door.

Isabella's heart took a leap and she placed the palm of her hand over her chest. Her face flushed with heat as she became as nervous as a child before a teacher.

The old man watched her walk up the stairs. She stood in front of the two French-styled doors with glass rectangles, covered on the other side by royal blue velvet curtains. She knocked gently.

The old man cupped his hands around his mouth and whispered loudly, "Go inside dear, go inside."

Isabella knocked again, then turned the knob slowly. The heavy door pulled open.

In front of her stood a petite, thin, hunchbacked old lady, wearing thin, round spectacles, magnifying her eyes to twice their size. Her hair was white as snow and pulled back very tight, then rolled up in a bun at back of her head, looking like a ball of white silk. Her nose was long and curved down and her lips were invisible on her tiny mouth. Her features were almost exactly the same as those of the cobbler downstairs, but more petite.

Her indigo blue dress danced on her skinny body. She stretched her very twiggy, wrinkly, white arms and reached for Isabella. Isabella stepped closer to her and replied by stretching out her own arms, letting her hands fall into the old lady's.

Isabella scanned the magic room, filled with bottles of all sizes and paintings of constellations on the wall, but the old lady pulled on her arms to bring her back to focus. She smiled. Isabella noticed her very large ears and smiled back at the old lady, thinking to herself how she reminded her of an elf or a gnome.

"What is your name, deary?" the old lady asked in a high-pitched voice.

"I am Isabella."

The old lady shook Isabella's hands in hers.

"Nice to meet you Isabella. I'm Pippa. I have been waiting for you. I must teach you all I know. The stars let me know you were coming. Soon I'll be a star too."

Isabella filled with excitement and regret, afraid she might not live up to Pippa's expectations.

"Tell me, deary," Pippa said, still holding Isabella's hands in hers. "Is your mother ill?"

Isabella's face became serious in surprise.

"Oh no, my mother hasn't even as much as caught a cold."

Pippa grasped Isabella's hands tighter. "You must go to her... then you must come back to me."

Isabella smiled and said, "But she is not ill, I assure you."

Pippa let Isabella's hands go and walked away slowly, saying, "Go, deary, go on... but do come back." Isabella left the room, walked downstairs and gestured to Samuel they must leave.

The old man, surprised by their quick exit, stopped what he was doing. "Leaving so soon?" he shouted.

Isabella turned around and shouted back as she entered the coach, "I'll be back!"

Chapter 33

Samuel and Isabella made it back to Fleurham. When the castle came into sight, Isabella noticed Maurice's horse and another horse and coach unknown to her.

Her stomach tightened up in knots and she began to sweat. Her legs shivered as Samuel pulled up, too slowly for her curiosity. "Hurry up Samuel, please. Pippa said Lilac would be ill." Samuel signaled the horses to speed up. The coach had barely come to a full stop when a nervous, jittery Isabella jumped out and ran inside the castle. Samuel ran behind.

As Isabella entered, she saw Bethlynn standing by the stairs. Puzzled, Bethlynn stared blankly at Isabella, who was scuttling her way to the stairs. Isabella heard men's voices coming from upstairs. She sprinted up quickly and recklessly, tripping over her dress as she noticed Maurice standing at the top waiting for her. Samuel and Maurice ran to help Isabella. Maurice pulled her up and held her hands as he looked in her eyes.

"What's happened to my mother?" she asked frantically, shaking.

"Your mother has fallen ill. The doctor is examining her now."

Isabella pulled herself away from her father's hold and ran up the stairs and down the hall, repeating loudly, "Oh my God, oh my God, oh my God." Maurice signaled for Samuel to wait downstairs. Isabella barged into the room and ran to Lilac's bedside, shoving into the fat man who was examining Lilac's face with his short, stubby fingers. Maurice quietly walked in after and stood at the foot of Lilac's bed, where she lay propped up with three fluffy pillows. Her golden hair was pulled back, displaying her unsymmetrical face completely.

Lilac looked at Isabella with tears in her eyes, but with no expression on her face. Her mouth was slanted down to one side, as was her right eye. She pointed to the doctor without saying a word.

"What's wrong, Momma?" Isabella asked.

Lilac pointed back at the doctor again.

Isabella looked at the fat, bald man for answers. He had moved back a few steps to give Isabella some space. He stared at Isabella, shocked to see a young woman behave so nervously and erratically. He dried droplets of sweat from his forehead and collar with a white handkerchief.

"Your mother has lost her ability to speak."

Isabella felt her heart drop and her eyes fill with quiet tears.

"What is wrong with my mother, doctor?"

The doctor walked to the window of the room and Isabella followed. He whispered, occasionally expelling spittle, causing Isabella to take tiny steps backwards as he spoke to her.

"Something went wrong in her brain, causing severe confusion and inability to speak."

Isabella held her stomach and crouched over, crying. "Will she be alright?" she asked in a low tone.

The heavyset doctor took a breath and paused. "We will have to wait and see."

Isabella ran to Lilac's side, crying, and crawled into the bed with her. "I'm sorry. I'm sorry for not having been the daughter you wanted.

This is my fault. I'm sorry. I love you, Momma."

Lilac's eyes welled up with tears as she had not called her momma for what seemed an eternity.

Isabella spent the rest of the day and night cuddled up to her mother.

Chapter 34

Early the next morning, Isabella headed back to see Pippa, leaving Lilac in the care of Maurice and Bethlynn.

Samuel waited in the coach as Isabella let herself out and scurried her way past the old cobbler and straight up the stairs to Pippa's study room. Isabella stood by the door shaking as Pippa slowly made her way to her.

"How is she, deary?" Pippa asked as she softly held Isabella's hands, noticing the bags and purple hues around her eyes.

"Something happened in her brain. She can't speak." Isabella replied, holding her tears back.

Pippa nodded. "Oh yes, yes. Cerebrum sanguis. It means 'brain blood' in Latin. Too much sadness... too much anger."

Isabella looked into Pippa's bright blue eyes and begged her, "Can you please tell me which remedy will cure her?"

Pippa let go of Isabella's hands and slowly walked back to her large wooden table stacked with charts, diagrams, and old books. She plopped herself into a large, weathered, brown leather chair that made her look like an infant in a giant's chair.

She began to sift through papers, muttering words in Latin with every sheet she turned. "Ah-ha! Hmm... hmm... hmm."

An excited Isabella walked and stood behind Pippa, who hummed as she tapped on a sheet with her long, skinny finger. "Ah... oh! The forbidden sed rutrum sapien."

Isabella hovered over Pippa, taking a close look at what she was reading.

"Why is it forbidden?" Isabella asked curiously.

"The plant is not forbidden. It is where it grows that is forbidden," Pippa whispered slowly in a mysterious voice, then jumped up out of her trance, startling Isabella.

"It's just as well... she can heal without the plant," Pippa said with a smile.

"Where does it grow? And why is it forbidden?" a frustrated Isabella asked.

Pippa added rhythm to her words and began to explain to Isabella as if telling a story to a child. "It is an enchanted forest. Anyone who enters will surely have to assume a debt to pay. Myth has it that the forest of Mulberry Hills is angry at being held captive, and anyone who enters will be punished."

Disillusioned, Isabella sighed, having heard this story before. She interrupted Pippa. "I will pay whatever it costs to give my mother her life back. It is my fault this happened to her."

Pippa shook her head from side to side and clicked her tongue in disapproval. "Dear, everyone has their own path in life, their own lessons to learn... You surely must never interfere with God's purpose. Deary, your mother does not belong to you. She is a child of God. Let His will be done."

Pippa continued to speak, but Isabella focused on memorizing the plant and location she saw in Pippa's diagram and ignored Pippa.

"Sit down, deary." Pippa said as she pointed at a small, worn-out wooden sofa.

Isabella walked around the desk and sat down slowly, sinking into the old, worn-out royal-blue cushion. Pippa walked over to her and placed her hands on her head. "Now pay close attention, young lady. This is how to heal the brain with your hands."

Pippa placed her skinny hands on Isabella's head, one hand on the crown and the other on the back. Softly she tapped over the crown of Isabella's head, moving the other hand segmentally from back to top, then side to side.

"The secret deary, is always in your imagination," Pippa said softly.

"How so?" Isabella asked.

"Every time your hand touches a section of the head, you will picture that part of the brain healing. Now, breathe in deeply, close your eyes, and feel."

Isabella became fascinated by the warm prickly feeling in her head as Pippa demonstrated. Pippa soon removed her hands from Isabella's head. "Now go on, deary. This is all she will need. Nothing else will be necessary."

Isabella jumped up and hugged Pippa's frail little body tightly. She released her gently and whisked out the door. "Be patient!" Pippa shouted as she watched Isabella run down the stairs and out of the house. "I will see you next week."

Chapter 35

Isabella arrived at the castle. She ran inside and straight to Lilac's quarters. She smiled, happy to see Maurice by her mother's side, comforting her.

"You will be alright. You are a strong woman," Maurice said to Lilac.

Lilac pulled herself up. She looked around the room, pointed at Isabella, and mumbled a sound, then lay back down. Maurice stepped back as Isabella approached her mother's side.

"I'm going to try to heal you, Mother," Isabella said as she placed her hands on Lilac's head.

Lilac took a deep breath and closed her eyes, allowing Isabella to have free reign of her body. As Isabella moved her hands around, she observed every inch of her mother's head. Her thinning blonde hair, the grey strands trying to integrate, her soft scalp. Isabella was reminded of Johndor's head, noticing how similar in shape and size they both were. She closed her eyes to redirect her focus back to Lilac's brain.

Isabella finished by placing her hand over her mother's heart. She felt her heart beat into her hand. Silently she thanked God her mother was alive.

Isabella stepped back to observe her mother's face. Lilac opened her eyes, smiled, and nodded yes. She pointed at Maurice.

"Now her," Lilac said.

Isabella smiled with joy. Maurice broke out in laugher, both that Lilac had spoken and that she had referred to him as a "her."

Bethlynn, who had secretly been peeking through the slit of the door, barged in. Excited to hear Lilac speak, she said to Lilac, "Let's hear more... surely there must be something you need to complain about."

"Alright," Lilac muttered.

The three waited anxiously for Lilac's next words. Lilac began, "Alright... alright... alright."

"Go on," Bethlynn said.

"Alright... alright." Lilac closed her eyes and began to snore. She mumbled non-sense in her sleep. "Bury... woods... curse... bury... bury... curse..."

Lilac had kept to herself the fact that Carmile never accomplished the last burial of the curse. According to Samuel, Carmile never answered her door the three times he attempted to take her to kill off the curse as Lilac had assigned him. The disappointment forever lived in Lilac.

A discouraged Isabella hung her head. Maurice moved close to Isabella and patted her head. "It's good progress. We must be patient," he said. He looked back at Isabella with a gentle gaze and said, "Keep working your magic."

Chapter 36

One week of Isabella tapping on her mother's head and Lilac regained her speech, but at a much slower pace. Isabella, frustrated that her mother was not the same, sought out Samuel, who was feeding the horses.

"Samuel, I need to go very, very early tomorrow. Before the sun rises. Inform no one."

Isabella headed directly into her study and opened up the chest of Johndor's arrows. She pulled them out one by one and placed them carefully on the floor next to her. She looked at the linen cloth hiding the cursed arrow. She put her hands under the cloth and lifted it out very carefully. She laid it slowly on the floor. Her hands began to sweat and her heart began to beat faster, as she was about to come face to face with the weapon that had ruled her life.

Nervously, she uncovered the flap. Flipping over one corner of the cloth, she exposed a silvery piece of metal. She unwrapped the rest of the cloth slowly, careful not to touch any part of the arrow, afraid it might bring harm to her.

She reached her head down to take a closer look. She examined every inch of the arrow, scratched and caked with sediment from the ground from twenty years ago, changing her idea of what it looked like in her mind's eye. She had imagined it black metal and much longer.

She wrapped it back up quickly and slid it under the small bed in the study. She put the other arrows away in the chest and put the chest away.

At 5:00 a.m. the next morning, Bethlynn walked into Isabella's quarters and shook Isabella's legs. "Wake up, Isabella." Isabella counted on Bethlynn's habitual early rising to wake her up early for her day's mission.

"I've packed a basket with buttered baguette and scones for you and Samuel." Bethlynn said. "Good luck with your apprenticeship today."

Isabella smiled nervously as her heart began to beat faster. She quickly dressed herself and walked downstairs. She looked up and down the hallway for Bethlynn before entering her study. She closed the door behind her quietly. She looked for her gardening tapestry bag and checked that her small shovel and pick were inside. She knelt down by the bed, slid out the arrow wrapped up in linen from under the bed and placed it in the bag. She quickly walked outside before Bethlynn could see her, forgetting the basket Bethlynn had prepared for the trip. She met Samuel waiting for her by the coach.

"Back to the Isle?" Samuel asked.

"North," Isabella said, pointing her shaky finger northward and rushing to get into the coach.

"North?" he asked, surprised.

"North!"

"North it is," he said under his breath, as he climbed on and took off northbound.

Samuel scratched his head in thought. North could only mean Cuvington. Perhaps she would visit the gravesite for Minna and Johndor. But why so early and by herself, he wondered. It didn't make sense to him and he felt somewhat uneasy at her suspicious and nervous demeanor.

Isabella recited to herself the location of the forbidden plant in a very low voice. "Between the tallest cedar and elm, between the tallest cedar

212

and elm." She shook her foot and twirled the two rings on her fingers with her thumb. She looked out the coach curtain in desperation. She began to talk to herself, rushing Samuel on their way before the sun rose completely and cocks began to crow.

She continued to recite the location of the plants until they finally reached Cuvington. She had not told Samuel where they were headed for fear he might refuse, but now she had to, as they were nearing Mulberry Hills.

Samuel slowed down. Isabella reached her head through the curtains and said, "Mulberry Hills, Samuel," and quickly stuck her head back in.

Samuel came to a complete stop.

Isabella poked her head through the curtains. "Samuel, we must move quickly before daylight. Please."

Samuel raised his voice in a very serious tone. "You do recall the fortress is prohibited, Isabella?" he asked as he moved the coach again, slowly.

Isabella did not respond or acknowledge his concern. She sniffed the cold morning air for the scent of mint. She noticed the burnt structure that marked the entrance to Mulberry Hills and the enchanted forest from a distance.

She scanned the top of the trees in search of a tall cedar tree and an elm tree. Samuel stopped directly in front of the gates where the sign prohibiting trespassers hung. Isabella jumped out and joined Samuel in the front.

"Keep going... slowly," she said as she looked forward and backward constantly.

"What are you looking for, Isabella?"

"The tallest cedar tree that stands next to the elm tree," she said slowly, concentrating her attention on the treetops.

Samuel pointed ahead. "I see an elm tree up ahead. But it seems to be..."

213

Isabella interrupted. "Where?" she asked excitedly, standing up for a better look. Samuel pointed.

"Over there. Seems to be deep in the woods. I don't think you'll..."

Isabella interrupted again. "There is the cedar next to it! Get closer to the gate." Suddenly, she doubled over, holding her stomach in pain.

"Are you alright?"

"I think I'm just hungry. I forgot to bring the basket." She tried to straighten up, but couldn't from the pain in her stomach. She climbed inside the coach again and sat crouched over. Samuel looked inside.

"Perhaps we should go back, Isabella. You don't look well."

"Give... me... a... minute... I'll... be... all... right... in... a... minute," she said, taking a breath between every word. Her long hair hung over her crouched body, her face against her knees.

"Isabella..."

"No Samuel, I must do this," she said, unraveling her body from the ball it had become. She pushed her hair behind her ears, exposing her pale face, with two pink spots marking where her knees had pressed.

She stepped out of the coach very slowly, still curved over, and shuffled her feet to the gate. Samuel held her arms to help her out. Tempted to remind her that her luck wasn't the best, instead he simply begged, "Please Isabella, don't."

Isabella walked to the gates, bent down, and crawled under. She tried to enjoy the enchanted trees and plants she could swear greeted her as she walked by them, but her discomfort was extreme.

She heard a strange sound, a harmonious high-pitched singing not familiar to her.

Out of nowhere, seven miniscule birds covered in glittery, silky, peach feathers flew around her. They dipped down close to her head and flew back up when she shooed them away.

She had never seen such beaks on birds—long tubular beaks that looked like petals of trumpet flowers. She kept walking, trying to not be distracted by the peculiar birds. She walked as fast as her pain allowed her.

She saw the cedar tree just a few feet to her left and the elm tree a few feet to her right and in between, different bushes. She looked around, desperately scouting out the one she had photographed in her mind. She spotted it and shuffled her way to a much smaller plant than she imagined. She knelt down and reached her hands out, grasping bushels of sed rutrum sapien. She whispered to the plant, "I honor your purpose for being. I ask permission to use you. Thank you."

Quickly, she pulled the branches out. She looked up and around, searching for the peculiar birds. They were nowhere to be seen or heard. She held the branches of the plant in her arms around her abdomen, still crouched over, and walked quickly back to Samuel. She stopped fast in her tracks when she noticed two French officials on horses speaking to Samuel. She hid behind a tree and waited for the men to ride off.

When they did, she ran into the coach and closed the curtains. Samuel rode off in the opposite direction from the French patrolling officials. No words were exchanged between Isabella and Samuel until they were outside the Cuvington boundaries. Isabella hid the plant and twigs in a white rag and stuffed them down her bustier.

Samuel, who was blatantly upset after being interrogated by one of the French officers, stopped the coach and pulled the curtain down behind him to speak to Isabella.

"I know I am to follow your orders, but with all due respect, Princess, I do refuse to ever bring you here again!" Isabella, feeling sheepish, let her head bow in shame.

"I'm sorry. Please don't tell. What did they want?" she asked timidly.

"How about... who was I? ... where did I come from? ... what did I come for at such an early hour?" Samuel answered her sarcastically.

"And what did you say?" she asked nervously.

"I told them I lost my way. I blamed a flock of strange, tiny birds for disrupting my attention." Isabella jumped up in excitement, as if she had not just committed an illegal act.

"Did you see them too?" she asked.

Samuel, still speaking sarcastically, said slowly, "I didn't know what scared me more, the birds, or the French officers riding up behind me at the same time." He looked back at Isabella. "Did you at least find what you needed?"

"Yes," she said, smiling with satisfaction. "Enough for Lilac and the herbal garden." Isabella looked at the tapestry bag sitting on the seat next to her. She grabbed it and carefully pulled out the wrapped arrow. She placed it on her lap, unfolding the cloth and staring intently at it. It gave her the feeling of an animal playing dead—perfectly still... yet menacing.

She was careful not to touch it with her bare fingers. She began to fear the change this act would bring. She feared that she would bury her identity with it. She was used to her cursed life. She had accepted that any chance of happiness would always be short-lived. She started getting cold feet as she identified herself more and more with the cursed arrow. She took a gulp. She was not ready. She became lost with the arrow for a moment, but then took one more look at it and felt a sense of rage rising up to her heart.

"You stole my life... my happiness," she whispered angrily. She wrapped the arrow back up and threw it back in the bag, ordered Samuel to stop, then quickly opened the coach door and jumped out, bag in hand.

"Since we are no longer in Cuvington, I am free to enter this small forest and gather more plants," she said assertively to Samuel as she dashed quickly into the forest. She walked along the edge of the woods, waiting for a sign of the perfect spot to bury the wretched arrow.

She swore she heard the peculiar high-pitched sound again. She looked up, but saw nothing around her but tall trees swaying their branches about. *It must be here,* she thought to herself.

She laid a large piece of cotton blanket over the ground and kneeled on it. She began to break up the dirt with a small hand shovel, then dug a wide hole about six inches deep. She pulled out the wrapped arrow and placed it, wrapped, into the hole. She filled the shovel with dirt and began to speak the words to reverse the cursed spell.

"Just as I bury you... the curse will break and be buried too."

She threw the first batch of dirt over the arrow as she began to hear the high-pitched sounds again. She stayed still to listen closer. She heard galloping. Afraid Samuel was coming closer, she put down the hand shovel and brought out from her bustier the white fabric full of sed ruprum sapien she had gathered from Mulberry Hills, trying to make it look as if she had just gathered it from this forest.

She ran to the edge of the forest, hoping Samuel would stop if he saw her coming to him with a handful of plants. Instead she saw the two French officers from Mulberry Hills approaching Samuel. She heard more galloping coming up behind her. She saw a man on a black horse, who slowed down as he saw the French officers gaining speed towards Isabella. The officers jumped off their horses and grabbed Isabella. Isabella, in a state of shock, could not speak. Tears rolled down her face. One of the men tore the plants out of her hands.

"Aha!" he said. "You are being arrested for trespassing and stealing at Mulberry Hills!" he continued in a thick French accent, as they pulled her by her arms. "We were watching you, Miss."

Samuel held his hands to his head, pleading with the two men. "Please sirs, she means no harm."

Isabella noticed the curious man on the black horse move behind a tree to hide from sight. He slowly moved in closer in order to take a better look, while still keeping his distance.

The taller French officer brushed his mustache with his fingers. "What is your name?" he asked aggressively. Isabella's head fell to her knees. She still could not speak.

Samuel answers for her. "Isa... Celeste. Her name is Celeste Inchaustegeaux, from Fleurham, sir."

"In you go, Inchaustegeaux," the French man said as he pushed her into the barred wagon attached to the horses. Isabella looked at him in despair with a solemn face and no emotion, as if her essence had been drawn out of her. She reached her hands out to Samuel and took off her two rings.

"Please Samuel... give these to Bethlynn. Tell her to take care of them for me." She held them tight and kissed them, then surrendered the rings to Samuel.

At this moment, the man on the black horse rode by, trying to look in the prisoner wagon, feeling that he knew Samuel and Isabella. *Having heard Samuel, however,* he thought to himself, *I have never known a Celeste,* and began to ride away, taking one last good look at Samuel as the two French men jumped on their shiny, twin brown horses and headed off with Isabella in the wagon.

After a few moments, the man on the black horse could not help his curiosity and returned to offer assistance to a very distressed Samuel, who had been pacing up and down with his head in his hands.

"Excuse me, sir," the man on the black horse said in a raspy voice, which sounded somewhat familiar to Samuel. "Celeste is her name?"

"Yes, Celeste... do you know her?" Samuel asked.

"No sir, I was just on my way to Fleurham and overheard her name."

"Fleurham! ... Fleurham! ... I've got to get back... I've got to get back," Samuel said, nervously running back to the coach and leaving the curious man behind.

The man walked to the site where Isabella had been digging, as he had noticed the blanket on the ground. He bent over to see what was in the hole. He pulled open the cloth with a piece of twig, being careful to not touch it. He leaned in to take a closer look. He touched the metal shaft and dug out the bit of dirt covering the other end of the arrow.

His heart beat fast and he pulled the arrow out of the ground. "Isabella!" he said out loud. He grabbed the half dressed arrow quickly and jumped on his horse, riding in the direction of the French officers until the wooden wagon came into view up ahead.

He slowed down and followed discreetly behind for the next 30 minutes into Cuvington. The two French officers rode around the gate into the prohibited area. The man on the black horse hid in a wooded area close by until he saw the French officers ride back out with no wagon attached. He waited for them to get far enough to be out of sight before he dared to ride into the restricted area. He saw a structure miles ahead. He rode back out and headed back to Fleurham.

He thought of a young Isabella the entire time as he headed back. As he approached the castle, he saw more French authorities outside the castle walls. They were confiscating plants in burlap sacks. As he got closer, he noticed they had destroyed what looked like a garden on the side of the castle. It was now bare, without a single plant, bush, or tree— just a mess of dirt all about the garden.

From a distance, the man on the black horse recognized an older Bethlynn, in tears, trying to reason with the officers. Samuel and Maurice were defending Isabella's attempt at helping her mother. The French authorities did not listen. They stacked up the sacks and rode away.

"Not a word to Lilac!" Maurice demanded.

The curious man on the black horse waited for the French authorities to leave before he came closer to the castle. He rode up to where Maurice, Samuel, and Bethlynn were gathered. They fell silent as he walked up to them. Bethlynn took a step back after studying his face.

"I know where they took her," he said.

Maurice, having never seen this stranger, asked, "And who might you be?"

The stranger answered Maurice respectfully. "I am William, sir," he said nervously, realizing it was the long-lost Maurice he was responding to.

Bethlynn took a deep breath. "The jeweler's nephew?"

"Yes," William said, as he held out a white velvet pouch. "I was on my way to deliver this piece to the queen when I saw them take Isabella... who is now Celeste?"

"Where is she?" Maurice asked.

"They have confined her in a prison in Cuvington. At nightfall, I will ride in and check on her," William said confidently.

Maurice jumped on his horse. "I will go reason with the French royals."

Bethlynn reached for the white velvet pouch. "I will take it to Queen Lilac," she said.

William held the pouch tight. "My apologies... I was instructed to deliver to the queen personally and make sure she looked at the piece."

"Yes, yes, of course," Bethlynn said, ushering him inside the castle.

"Was that her healing herbal garden they destroyed?" William asked. Bethlynn nodded in disappointment.

"She put so much love and effort into building it. It was her passion and her happiness. And now... it is gone." She paused. "I must warn you... Lilac has fallen ill and has recovered only just."

William indicated that he understood with a nod of the head. "I will be brief."

William and Bethlynn walked into the sitting room, where Lilac sat sipping slowly on tea and scoffing down biscuits. Her forms of satisfaction were often contradictory to one another.

Lilac looked at William, not recognizing him. "Who... is... that?" she asked Bethlynn, pausing between every word.

"This is William. Orlette, the jeweler's nephew... remember?"

"Oh, is that right?" Lilac replied with more enthusiasm in her voice.

Bethlynn continued. "She has sent something for you to look at with her nephew WILLIAM," putting emphasis on his name so as to jog Lilac's memory.

"What a handsome man you turned out to be. How is Orlette?"

William began to answer. "Her feet seem to be a prob..."

Lilac interrupted. "Does Celeste know you are here? Celeste! Celeste!" she called out.

"Celeste is not here at the moment, Lilac." Bethlynn answered with a fake smile. "Show her quickly," she whispered to William in order to distract Lilac from asking about Isabella.

William handed Lilac the white pouch. She tried to unravel the silk string with her weak hands. She looked at Bethlynn and whispered, "Go get Celeste."

"Right away," Bethlynn said facetiously as she walked away, winking at William.

Lilac handed the pouch back to William, not having been able to untie it. "Please William, do me the honor."

He quickly untied the cord and pulled out a gold ring with a large rectangular ruby stone, which had been broken into a triangular shape.

"My ring!" Lilac said loudly. "Oh, my ring... my ring," she said, excitedly. She tried to place her long-lost wedding ring on her left ring finger. It was tight, but she found the strength to push it all the way on to her finger. Her eyes teared up as she stretched her fingers slowly and stared at the ring.

"How did she find it?" Lilac asked in a slow, cracking voice.

"A passerby peasant from Nokbershire claimed he found it. Aunt

Orlette recognized it immediately. She offered him a petty amount for it, and he accepted." William explained.

"I will surely pay her back generously."

"She demands no payment. It is an honor for her to be able to return to you what is rightfully yours," he said.

Lilac held up her hand and stared at the ring sadly, noticing the cracked ruby. "Broken, like my marriage," she whispered to herself. She turned to William and smiled. "It's a family heirloom, you know. It was Maurice's grandmother's wedding ring. I wished to one day hand it down to Isa... Celeste."

William became serious as he stared at the ring intently.

"Is there something wrong, William? You seem worried."

"I didn't realize the ring was damaged. It is quite a shame. I would like to have it repaired for you and make it a tad larger to fit your finger more comfortably. With your permission, may I take it back and fix it for you? I promise I will return with it. You have my word."

Lilac twisted and twisted the ring until it came off her finger. She then placed it in the white pouch. "Here you go... it also means you will return to see my Celeste."

William secured the white pouch in his leather vest and bowed his head. Lilac waved her hand to dismiss him as he quickly backed out of the room.

"My regards to Orlette."

As William reached the hallway, he pulled the ring out of the pouch. He brought it close to his eyes, observing where the piece of the ruby stone was missing. What was supposed to be a rectangular ruby was now a triangle. He felt the stone with his finger. The corners that had held the missing piece of ruby were lifting and scratched the pad of his finger. He took a deep breath, secured the ring in the pouch and put it back in his vest as he headed out of the castle in a rush.

Chapter 37

William rode off in the direction of Cuvington and waited in a wooded area for the day to be dark enough to obscure him. He was confident he would not be seen in his black garments and that his jet-black horse would camouflage him against the dark sky.

He rode around the gates at Mulberry Hill and raced towards the structure to which he had seen the French officers take Isabella. He constantly looked in all directions for any signs of officers. He tied his horse to the closest tree and carefully walked quickly to the grey brick structure. He examined the small building from a distance for any windows or doors and noticed a small window on the far side with metal bars. Excitedly, he ran towards the window, tripping over a large stone and falling flat on his face. He slowly stood up and walked carefully towards the window.

Surely there must be a door, but it is too dark to see it, he thought to himself. *I've no time to waste,* he thought, as he slowly slid his face along the wall until he could see through the corner of the small window.

Suddenly he saw a skinny face with black, straggly hair jump in front of him on the other side of the window.

"What do you want?" she whispered loudly in a scratchy, high-pitched voice.

William jumped back, startled, taken aback by the woman's sudden appearance and witchy looking face. Her thinning, black and gray hair framed her long, wrinkled, skinny face.

William quickly moved back to the window. "I'm looking for somebody," he whispered.

"For me?" she said, pointing at her chest. "Oh no, not for me. Why? What more do you want from me? Are you going to hang me? Are you going to burn me at..."

William interrupted in a loud whisper. "No! No!"

She continued to ramble nervously. William tried to interrupt her again. "No... I'm not going to... what is your name?" he asked assertively.

She quieted down and stepped back, then slowly walked back to the window. "Feralia," she said slowly. "My name is Feralia."

William put his hands up, palms facing her, and spoke slowly. "I am not going to harm you... I am not looking for you." Feralia came closer to the window, searching for other people outside.

"How many more are in there?" William asked. Feralia stretched out four shivering fingers.

"Four... NO! ... Five! They've just brought in a witch... the weeping witch. That's what Guilamina calls her." She chuckled, covering her mouth.

"Tell me their names!" William demanded.

"No... no... you will harm them," Feralia said.

William, growing angrier, raised his voice. "TELL... ME... THEIR... NAMES!"

Feralia trembled, pointing at herself. "Feralia," she said, her voice shaking and cracking. She held up another finger. "Shamantha." She held up a third finger. "Guilamina." She held up her small finger. "Anghrella." She popped up her thumb. "And the weeping witch."

William cocked his head to the side, trying to be patient. "Feralia, what is her name... the weeping witch?" Feralia shook her head from side to side nervously.

"I don't know, I don't know. But you should take her. Guilamina said it is because of witches like her that we are here."

"I want to see her," William said gently, yet sternly. "Where is she?"

Feralia tapped her chest and gasped loudly for air, as if she had heard something absurd. She pointed down at the floor. William pulled himself up, holding on to the bars. He looked down at the floor and saw nothing but Feralia's dirty bare feet. Her dry, cracked skin and long, dirty toenails repulsed him and he pulled himself back down, took a breath, and pulled himself back up.

"Where is she, Feralia?" he asked again, aggressively.

Feralia pulled herself close to the small opening and whispered. "She's under," she said, pointing down, "in the dungeon."

"Go get her!" William demanded.

"No! No! No!" Feralia said, adamantly shaking her head from side to side.

"GO NOW!" William yelled with a loud whisper, as he let himself down and searched for the stone he had tripped over.

Feralia stepped back quickly and pulled her hair back, combing it with her fingers. She patted her cheeks nervously as if to make sure she could feel. Slowly, she bent down on her knees and slid a large brick square forward, displaying a square opening. She held onto the edges and put her head through.

"Witch girl!" she whispered loudly. "Witch girl!"

William carried the heavy stone over, placed it under the window, and climbed on top of it, giving himself a full view inside of the structure. He whispered loudly, "Go down and get her, Feralia!"

"Oh... no... no... no! It's dark down there. I can't breathe and the stairs... no... no!"

William took a deep sigh to calm himself. He heard Feralia whisper loudly, "Wait... she comes." Feralia's head dipped back into the hole on the floor. "Be careful... watch your step... hold up your dress, careful not to step on your dress. Hold on tightly..." Feralia stood up quickly and brushed off her own dress as Isabella pulled herself out of the opening.

"What is it?" Isabella asked. Feralia covered her mouth with one hand and pointed to the window. Isabella took a step towards the opening. Feralia yanked Isabella's arm and pulled her back.

"Be careful... keep your distance," she whispered.

Isabella came into William's view. He took a deep breath. His heart sank with sadness and at the same time beat faster with excitement.

"Fix your hair," Feralia said nervously, combing her long, dirty fingers through Isabella's hair, then clasped her hands in front of her and twiddled her thumbs nervously.

Isabella saw William at the window. She did not recognize him. As she stepped closer, he called her name, but she still did not recognize the handsome, black-haired man.

"China doll... it's me... William."

Isabella ran to the window in tears. She cried with desperation and shame in her voice. William reached for her shaky hands through the bars and held them in his. He kissed her fingers as she cried.

"I never thought I would see you again," Isabella whimpered.

William tried to reach in closer, but the opening was too small. He gently turned her head sideways, reached toward her ear, and whispered, "Worry about nothing... I am here now." Isabella turned her head slowly, sliding her cheek against his mouth. As she pulled away, she looked at him, confused by his expression of affection.

"I must go before I am seen, but I will be back," William said.

He stepped down from the stone, moved it a few feet away from the structure, and ran back to his horse. Isabella smiled with a sense of hope as she watched him leave. Feralia walked to her and spoke quickly. "He won't come back you know... he won't. They will probably hang you before he comes back... if he ever does..."

Isabella's smile became a frown as she fell to her knees and cried into her hands.

Chapter 38

Isabella sat by the window all day long and laid herself to sleep under the window at night for the next week. The other women joined Isabella by the window in the event that William indeed showed up. She felt a crippling fear that, as her luck would have it, he might not come back to see her.

Nighttime had come and a dismayed Isabella lay silent, facing the wall, her body curled up in the fetal position, shivering mildly from the cold drafts entering through the window. Her hair fell over her face and her toes curled tight under the skirt of her dress. She stared at the stone brick squares before her and picked at the crevices with her fingertips, not realizing that William had returned to Cuvington that day just before the sun began to set and was hidden as he watched for the French officers to desert the jail premises.

"That's just your luck," Anghrella, one of the prisoners, told her as she sat on the floor by Isabella's head. "Stop waiting for him; he won't come back for you." Guilamina and Shamantha, a set of twins, sat close to Anghrella and pestered Isabella.

"You tried to heal your mother and now you'll never see her again," Shamantha said sadly.

"Not too smart, are you?" Guilamina chimed in condescendingly.

Shamantha slid closer to Isabella. "You must feel terrible," she said sympathetically, patting Isabella's hand with compassion.

Guilamina and Shamantha's faces were almost identical, except in the eyes. Guilamina's eyes were brown and wide. Shamantha's were small and blue with drooping eyelids. Guilamina was heavyset and stood up straight, while Shamantha was thin, with slouched posture, and she was not as sharp as her sister.

Isabella spoke weakly and tapped the wall as she defended herself to the women. "I was only trying to cure my mother."

"IT'S STILL ILLEGAL!" Anghrella screamed, holding up her hands to her flushed face.

Guilamina laughed and said, "It's still illegal, weeping witch... illegal."

Shamantha repeated, "Illegal, illegal, illegal," as she played with Isabella's hair.

Feralia, who stared out the window vigilantly, nudged Isabella with her foot. "Illegal, weeping witch." The four women joined in laughter, mocking Isabella.

Isabella took a deep breath, rolled over in a flash, and stood up, her face red with anger. "Quiet! All of you... quiet!" she yelled as she looked at each of them. They backed up one by one, shocked at Isabella's response. Shamantha held her sister's hand and hid behind her larger body.

Her voice softening, Isabella continued, "We are all in here together. Let's help each other instead." She walked to Feralia and held Feralia's hands in hers and looked softly in her eyes. She said gently, "Don't be so afraid of everything, Feralia. Everything will turn out alright."

Feralia's eyes welled up with tears as she reached her arms out and hugged Isabella. "Are you sure?" Feralia whispered in Isabella's ear.

"I promise," Isabella whispered back. Isabella then turned to Guilamina and Shamantha. She put Guilamina's hand in Shamantha's.

Guilamina tried to break the grasp. Isabella held their hands together.

"Don't forget who you were before you came here. You are both good women." Guilamina looked down. Shamantha nodded.

"Yes, yes we are."

"We all made mistakes, but that is all. It is a mistake. You are not a mistake," Isabella said assertively.

Shamantha repeated her, laughing with joy. "We are not a mistake, we are not a mistake." Guilamina followed with laughter.

Isabella then looked at Anghrella, who had stood up and was pacing up and down, trying to resist Isabella's encouraging words. Anghrella was too tall for Isabella to look her in the eyes. "Please sit with me, Anghrella," Isabella said.

Anghrella stared at Isabella silently, afraid Isabella might break her down emotionally. She slid down the wall slowly until her bottom hit the floor. Isabella knelt in front of her, holding Anghrella's face to keep her from turning her head.

"I don't know what happened to you, but it is over. Let it go."

Anghrella took a deep breath and looked up. She grabbed her blonde hair, chopped so short that it looked like dried straw, and squeezed her fists tightly. She let out an infuriated yell and fell onto Isabella's shoulder, sobbing uncontrollably. Shamantha and Guilamina knelt down and hugged Anghrella and Isabella. Feralia walked around the women, nervously trying to find a spot where she could join in the hug. Isabella pulled her down gently by her hand and Feralia giggled skittishly.

Isabella sneezed, breaking up the hug and sending Feralia running to the other side of square brick room. Feralia covered her nose and mouth. "Don't make me sick. I don't want to die. I don't want to die in here," she said, her voice muffled under her hand.

Anghrella's pulled the large brick covering the stone steps. "We will all get sick if we continue to sit by the window," she said as she climbed down the opening on the floor. "Chop-chop," she said, her voice echoing from inside the chamber, demanding the other ladies come down.

Isabella looked in all directions out the window, sneezed loudly, and made her way to the opening. She held her dress up with one hand and stepped through carefully. Guilamina and Shamantha followed. Feralia, still covering her nose and mouth, went last, sliding the stone brick to cover half of the opening.

Thirty minutes after the ladies had made their way down and prepared to sleep, William arrived at the structure. He sought out the stone and carried it close to the window. He stood up and looked inside the empty room. He whispered loudly, "Isabella! Isabella!" He waited, then called out for Feralia. He waited, continuously calling out their names. He walked around the tall structure searching for a door. The pitch-black night made it impossible to see. He returned to the window and examined the fire sconces that were strategically only placed on the wall of the window. They were too high to reach. He pulled his horse close and climbed on its back as he supported himself with the bars of the window. He stretched his arms up as he propped himself up on the tips of his toes, then toppled off and landed on his back, letting out a loud grunt. He lay on the ground for a minute as the pain throughout his body subsided. He slowly walked to the window, climbed on the stone and took a last look inside. Holding his lower back, he climbed on his black horse and rode slowly into the forest. He found a soft spot on the ground and laid his aching body down.

Chapter 39

The next morning, just before the break of dawn, while the skies were still dark, the two French guards rode to the structure where the ladies were confined. Feralia, who slept close to the door, heard the clanking of the metal keys and the voices of the two men. She crawled quietly to Anghrella and shook her shoulder.

"Wake up, the officers are coming," Feralia said, her voice breaking. "They never come while we sleep. They're going to hang us! They're going to hang us!" she said as she started crying.

Anghrella sat up slowly as she rubbed her eyes open. "Are you having a nightmare again, Feralia?" she asked, waking the other girls.

"Shhh," Feralia said, covering Anghrella's mouth with her skinny, bony hand. Guilamina stood up quickly, putting her ear to the door. Isabella's heart beat faster, and she felt short of breath. Shamantha ran to Isabella and held her hand.

"What are they here for, do you think?" Isabella asked nervously. Feralia rubbed her neck with her hand as she hid behind Anghrella. Guilamina and Anghrella stood close to the door.

Isabella shed a quiet tear. "If they take me, I will never see William again." She made her way quietly up the stairs, tempted to hide on the upper floor. The women became even more anxious and jittery at hearing the key turn, unlocking the door. They stepped back in fear as they watched the door open slowly. Isabella took another step up the stairs.

A tall, thin man dressed in blue stepped in. He brushed his manicured salt-and-pepper moustache and said loudly, in a thick French accent, "Out! Let's go!" as he pointed to the other French officer, who stood holding the door open.

Guilamina, who was closest to the door, walked out quickly, calling out to her sister. "Shamantha! Let's go!" Shamantha looked up at Isabella. Isabella took two more steps up and gestured to Shamantha to go. Guilamina shouted again at Shamantha and Shamantha ran out behind her sister. Feralia walked behind Anghrella, still holding her neck with one hand and the back of Anghrella's purple dress with the other. Isabella ran up and looked out the window for any sign of William.

The second French guard yelled at the women, "Into the box... Dans la boîte!" gesturing for them to enter the same wagon they were brought in. The tall, thin guard took one more look around the empty cell and walked out behind the ladies.

Isabella watched from the window as the four ladies were taken away. She cried as the distance shrank them from her sight. She crouched on the floor and sobbed.

William had been awakened by the trotting of the officer's horses, and was watching from the forest. He noticed a coach and horses waiting at the gates. He quickly rode and approached a young French officer who stood waiting by the coach, nibbling on a piece of baguette.

"From around here?" William asked, pretending to be lost.

"No," the young officer said with a heavy French accent. "Just on service," he said, brushing the crumbs away from his chin.

"What kind of service?" William asked.

"Just transporting the young ladies that have been freed back to their village. Good day for them."

"Good day for them, indeed." William said as he rode back to the forest, seeing the two French officers arriving with the ladies. He stayed close enough to get a good view of the ladies as they were let out of the prison wagon. Anghrella dared to ask the tall thin French man where they were being taken.

"*La liberté*... freedom!" the man shouted assertively. "Now go quickly into the chariot that is waiting... quickly... go... go!"

Anghrella walked fast and entered the coach. Shamantha held her hands close to her heart in prayer, waiting for Feralia, who was the last to enter the coach.

William rode closer. Not seeing Isabella, his hopeful heart sank. The coach rode off and the officers rode behind. Feralia stretched her head out the window to feel the wind on her face. She caught a glimpse of William as they rode by the forest. She stuck out her hand and pointed at the structure, letting him know Isabella was still in there.

He watched and waited for the French officers to be far off in the distance and then he raced to the structure at such a fast speed, he resembled a large black arrow in the air. He reached the structure and jumped off his shiny black horse. He pulled on the small brick door, which had been left open.

He called for Isabella.

She cringed in fear, thinking the men had come back for her, although she knew they always referred to her by her surname, Inchaustegeaux, and she was being called by her first name this time.

William called for her again. He noticed the stairs hidden in a dark nook by the back wall. He climbed up, pushing the brick out of the way. He saw Isabella lying on the floor, sobbing. "Isabella," he said, making his way through the hole.

She crawled her way to him, helping him through the hole, and falling into his arms, shaking. "Why did you stay behind?"

Isabella pulled away from his shoulder and dried her face.

"I was afraid they would hang me. I hid up here."

"All the ladies have been freed, and so have you," William said, smiling. Isabella shook her head from side to side in disbelief.

"The others are free, but I am not. I just got here. They will only bring me back."

"Why would they free the others and not you? Be sensible, Isabella," he said.

"Because it is my luck!" she yelled, crying. "Because I am cursed!"

"Isabella, please let me see your scar," William said, pulling her dirty white linen dress slowly up to her knees. She stopped crying and watched him attentively as he pulled the leather bag over his head and laid a long leather pouch on the floor. He unwrapped it and pulled out the cursed arrow Isabella was attempting to bury the day she was caught.

Isabella gasped. "Don't touch it!" she yelled. William grabbed the arrow firmly with his bare hands.

"This piece of metal is not going to harm me," he said assertively. He held the tip of the arrow close to her scar. She moved her leg away quickly. He grabbed her leg and pulled it back to him. She relaxed at his secure and protective demeanor. He placed the arrow tip next to the scar, comparing the size and shape. He laid the arrow down on the floor and pulled out the white velvet pouch with Lilac's broken ring. He placed the ring next to Isabella's scar and then over the scar. The three marks on Isabella's leg matched up perfectly to the edges of the broken ruby of Lilac's ring. He looked deeply into Isabella's eyes—a look she felt in the core of her soul.

Isabella looked down, sliding the ring away from her scar and then back over the scar again, fitting it like a missing puzzle piece. William brought his mouth close to hers. "You, my darling, have never been cursed."

Their lips met and they fell into a deep, long-awaited kiss. Isabella felt a heavy weight release from her body, filling her heart with deep joy.

William secured the ring in his vest and the arrow in its pouch. He lifted Isabella's light body and carried her down and out of the structure. He lifted her onto his horse and shoved the arrow victoriously into the ground. Climbing onto his horse, they rode off into the sunrise.

The smell of freedom captured Isabella's senses. She inhaled deeply as she heard Thumbeline's voice echoing through the trees. "The things we believe, that is the real curse."

About the Author

C.V. Shaw is the author behind *The Spell*. She is a great believer in magic and imagination. She is a doctor of Oriental medicine and a quantum energy practitioner. She specializes in herbology, Reiki, hypnosis, sacred and bio geometry, medical qigong, craniosacral therapy, and alpha intuitive healing. She is also a MindScape instructor. A native South Floridian, C.V. Shaw's alternative medicine practice is located in South Miami. She has published work in *How to Survive Your Teenager* and *Story Circle Journal*. As a journalist, she was a feature writer for M.D. News, Florida Medical Business, Miami Herald Neighbors, and Club Systems International. C.V. Shaw's short story *Looped* was shortlisted in *Retreat West UK* writing competition.

C.V. Shaw loves to hear from her readers.

Follow her on (f) (◎) @cvshawbooks and www.cvshawbooks.com

CPSIA information can be obtained
at www.ICGtesting.com
Printed in the USA
LVHW012336061121
702609LV00003B/15

9 780997 290486